T0096664

Shortlisted for the John Llewellyn Rhys Prize, Rebbecca Ray published her first novel, *A Certain Age*, when she was eighteen and released her second, *Newfoundland*, to critical acclaim in 2005. *The Answer and Other Love Stories* is her first work for eight years.

She lives in Mid Wales with her growing family.

The Answer
and Other Love Stories

The Answer

and Other Love Stories

Rebbecca Ray

Parthian
The Old Surgery
Napier Street
Cardigan
SA43 1ED

www.parthianbooks.com

First published in 2013
© Rebbecca Ray 2013
All Rights Reserved

ISBN 9781908946928

Editor: Kathryn Gray
Cover by www.theundercard.co.uk
Typeset by Elaine Sharples
Printed and bound by Gomer Press, Llandysul, Wales

Published with the financial support of the Welsh
Books Council

British Library Cataloguing in Publication Data

A cataloguing record for this book is available
from the British Library.

Contents

The Answer

For Edward Lowe

This is a story concerning London, the proud capital city of a first world country, and a few of the people who live there.

It begins late in the evening, on a night of sadness for one in particular. For although he's still surrounded by others, Stanley Parsons is non-operational, yet to embark upon his journey, and as lonely as a question mark.

DAY # 0

Someone is dying – and say that in the other room you're seeing through the window this night sky. It's summer – August, say. The normal, practical things of life, the biscuit tins and bus stop views and tiling jobs of life are still the same, but in the middle is this ending. The world does not embody what you feel but continues to be: mundane and useless and unbelievable. Someone is dying. The person with whom you've spent your whole life. A car is passing. The television is audible from next door. Perhaps it's an advert for private health care.

In Archway, the fire began. He stood on the garden path while their bedroom windows flickered softly. The engines' warning lights lapped the pavements and fighters filled their home. The battle had been silent in there for months but tonight, at neighbours' windows, faces appeared – unafraid of flames, which couldn't creep up on you in the same way that throat cancer could. Between the flowerbeds, he stood like a drowning tree in this activity. Men had rushed from one vehicle with a plastic whiteboard and, kneeling on the grass verge beside their garden wall, had written into a column Stanley and Claire's address. This was where he'd been told to wait, here in the centre of the world. They had it all in hand.

It was interesting because he'd had no one to help him before. A week last Thursday Claire had come from the hospital. Stanley had had numbers of course – emergency

7

numbers – but what could they have assisted him with? They'd come and changed her, perhaps ten minutes a day, but really their jobs had been done. He was told to call afterwards and they would come to certify it. For a few days at the end of life, the system fled and let nature take over.

Now, a strangely silent scene. No alarms – the voices of curiosity could be heard, just twenty yards, fifty yards down the road.

Stanley was supposed to remain in this spot until the Fire Investigation Team arrived. He'd told people already, but it just didn't sound good:

'My wife died of cancer. Then the TV exploded and the living room burnt down.'

If there'd been doubts, the firemen themselves hadn't voiced them; they'd conceded, televisions burned hotter than mostly everything. And it wasn't that he didn't want to help them find answers. Questions were rampant though, they ate up normality. There was no stopping them now his wife was dead. For instance this:

The way they had been cheated. Throughout life they had made decisions based, not really on what they wanted, but on what would bring them security. Claire had been four months from retirement though; security was a lie. No one could offer it to you, not for the highest premiums in the world. And if security was an illusion – plans and savings and added equity, bungalows and a national health system and the contributions that paid for it, and all the slow steps of promotion she'd taken, and all the Amway products on which they'd never make their money back, and God, as everyone who'd ever tried to bring this their way had ever presented it, and atheism too, for what had that brought them? – if everything they'd been surrounded by was a sham in the presence of this death, then what was real?

Questions had no borders.

It wasn't just grief but fear and anger. Before him was this street, which he recognised, and the lights of the city beyond. Shops sparkled there, Sainsbury's Locals, and buses circled with the endless beeps of commuters charged and counted, teenagers grouped around Chicken Spot and Good Chicken and Chicken Cottage while overhead security cameras slowly changed rotation. Throughout the sodium-yellow summer night, customers wandered between bright, open doorways, talking about new films or distant disasters, about politics, relationships in their workplaces or sport, and hardly thought of death at all.

Part of the problem Stanley faced now was the *way* that Claire had died; with black unidentified liquid coming out of her mouth and backing up through the pipes in her stomach and nose, covering their lilac towel set one by one. He had lived in the world for fifty two years and nothing had prepared him for it.

Streets, he saw, night fields of them. You could see more of London from Highgate Hill than anywhere and you couldn't see the ends of it.

The whole problem, the problem in its entirety, occupied Stanley's soul and stopped him believing – in anything he saw. He must stand here now and wait, yes this was what he'd been told, for though there had been no one to stand and help him change the towels under

Claire's cheek, there was an entire Team to interview him about what had happened afterwards. He didn't want to answer questions. They had joined hands – every question that ever existed – and the chain they had formed encircled the world. If they could be put back into their boxes, separate, *then* he would be able to return – speak to the Fire Investigation Team. By that point maybe they'd be able to make some sense of this together. At the moment he couldn't find anything that seemed solid. And he couldn't just – what? – continue?

The world rang with this sound

–

and made him realise that he was powerless. He couldn't shout now to make anyone hear him. Even these men, who were trying to save what they could of the house behind him, wouldn't have understood if he'd called out like he needed to, just to ask to be heard, to make every one of them realise that it would happen to them, the people they loved would die, and they themselves and one day their kids. Everyone. If lives were tiny lights then London would have been transcendent with their glittering revolutions.

In fact, London's lights would be constant again tonight, all across Kentish Town and Camden and down, through the West End or in Canary Wharf's silver courtyards, until the sensors detected daybreak. Stanley now worked as a security guard, though he'd taken a great deal of time off recently. Over the course of the five years he'd been doing the job, a sensation had gradually become clearer, a discomforting sensation. This time of year dawn was silent in Canary Wharf and silence was frightening in such a well-lit place.

Stanley Donald Parsons looked out now and that sensation was the concrete truth. Yet he couldn't articulate it to anyone. In fact, there was nothing he could do at all. One person couldn't make the world stop, not even for a single moment.

No, one person could only stop themselves.

Stan Parsons must simply refuse to go on being.

He must utterly cease. Stand fast, do nothing, absolutely nothing, refuse to cooperate in any way with life, and answer no questions of theirs until he understood his own. SDP (as his friends used to call him when they'd all been very young) would discontinue.

Let the world see how it would deal with that one.

No one prevented him. He opened the garden gate without thought of the car and his feet just propelled him away. He wasn't homeless: there it stood, behind him, growing smaller, with its blackened window frames and busy doorway. He wasn't yet accused of any crime. He wasn't mentally ill. He would have described it – that night as he sat and drank on the pavement of Junction Road, he did describe it to himself – as an illness of the heart, a realisation. They'd been conned.

They'd conned themselves.

Look:

DAY # 1

Pizza. On a roll.

It's an incredible idea.

The sign has been lit all night.

This street's slight-broken silence is the sound of everything outside his life. He's never seen the place like this before. He's on leave, in a foreign land.

Pizza. On a roll.

He's no longer a security guard, nor a carer anymore. In the cold air, the flutter of loose threads.

Outside the newsagents, last fluoro lighting fades against a coldwater sky. Unable to go home without having to account for what happened.

A police car went by last night, around four, with a ghost's passage, and neither of the occupants looked at him.

Listen to that, Claire, he thinks – though he knows she can't.

There are these *tiny* morning sounds – like a bird.

This is Archway and Stanley is looking at Junction Road, flowing wide and still and changeless past his feet to the intersection that gives it its name: Highgate Hill, the Holloway Road, St John's Way, Archway Road. No one is up but the cleaners this time of day.

He can't account for anything.

If they'd seen what he had then they just would have stood there staring at the living room going up as well – the world had desperately needed, just in that one small area, to burn.

He doesn't want the whole world to burn; he's not an anarchist. In general he has always liked the place, with its many perfectly nice people – in some ways all the wars are unaccountable. Perhaps he's been naïve. Maybe the world's never shown him its true colours.

What is he to make of that though? He has lived here, with everybody else. His hasn't been a sheltered life, particularly. And yet no one had described to him – nowhere had he ever read or seen televised, never had he heard anyone talk about death in the way he's just seen it. Claire had wanted to die at home and he had wanted it too but he hadn't understood.

It was as if the world kept this secret. Their living room had felt a closeted place – and yes, the curtains had always been drawn in the end. In how many other homes, Stanley wondered, were people dying in this secret way? Unsupported. Moving the sofas back three feet to make sick rooms out of lounges. We hadn't progressed really. Where was the progression? Though Les Dennis played endlessly on the television in the corner and your home was full of such modern medical equipment as to replace the role of every working body part, you were only waiting. The equipment was only to assist in waiting. It held the body in place while it broke down. You shut the curtains to hide this from the rest of the world because it was frightening. Because we'd progressed in a lot of other areas.

(Pizza. On a roll.)

Surely these days people didn't have to die so nastily?

What is he saying?

He's hungry. His wallet is on the kitchen counter beside the protein drinks that Claire was unable to take for the last two weeks. He can picture it unscathed, but also burnt. And the Nestlé Milo? There's a cartoon boy on the front, hurdling. Maybe unable to hurdle anymore.

He won't go back for it. He has never had cause to dislike money but this morning the thought of walking home to pick it up makes him feel nauseous. Makes him hate the world, in a way he isn't prepared for.

He will sit here. He will watch it get light.

He glances around the abandoned high street. Archway's a Mecca for bargains; Stella, cat food, Turkish bread, kebabs, heroin. Though the street's wide and holds a lot of sky, it's not a place for star gazers. At night the air is milky. People pass through here in patterns – like the constellations – but to a city's schedule. People pass through but few of them stay. There aren't any real handholds here. They can get a meal at two am but not past then.

Only one twenty four hour shop. Perhaps they'll give to him. He won't steal food.

Across a whole portion of the world morning is taking place. Strong sun is touching Europe and the Mediterranean, glinting from each high and tiny jet plane. In the south it's

14

winter now, in another hemisphere, but still every clock tells the time agreed. Day is on its way, boxing the compass.

In Archway, the first hour opens. The beginning of the regular flow of buses. This is not a beautiful street.

Quiet is gradually stolen away by the early men, smoking second or third cigarettes – delivery drivers, council workers, operators, guards, coming to take their places at each joint of the infrastructure.

This is a good time for insomniacs to go shopping. You'll see them crisply closing front doors with last night's dreams still out of reach. Children are waking up to Radio One, with chocolate cereals and revision and slowly solidifying ideas of hierarchy. People searching for a home in this city are dialling numbers from classified ads and looking at a world of drawn curtains for which contracts have already been signed. On *Newsbeat*, thirty four have died in a suicide bombing, President Bush has detailed plans to return to the moon and it's been discovered that there's a gene for ambition.

Around the unattended baggage of Stanley Donald Parsons, here comes normal life.

Throughout all the mornings of the world, the homeless people are awake. They're homeless in parks and doorways, in derelict buildings, on pavements and on the verges of Drive-Thrus, in cars. They sit under varying skies; above the days go by unnamed. Everywhere you go the end of the world is not nigh.

The pavement is still cold, though it looks like it'll be a summery day. Stan sees the odd cigarette butt, but he doesn't smoke – not anymore.

What does he do?

How did it come to this?

He's always been part of the majority. He shouldn't be tool-less, lost. He can't believe what a surprise it's all been. He looks around and death is an anomaly.

Everything works so well. The world Stanley sees has no gaps in it. If people were dying left, right and centre, it wouldn't look like this. There would be signs.

Cancer can be invisible for quite a long time. Claire's illness 'began' on the 25th of October with a bottle of Sunny Delight. Stan found her in the kitchen, hand to her throat, choking on it. When she'd been able to speak again her voice had sounded strange. She'd talked about how much the stuff had hurt her. He can't believe, in retrospect, that he let it go unnoticed as a warning sign.

Claire had been Access Development Manager for a strategy firm in Mudchute. Job stress over the first two months had masked the weight-loss and fatigue. Most of all they should have noticed her constant tiredness. By February she'd been unable to make it through a team meeting without leaving for some respite – she'd sat outside on the edge of the antique barrel that held flowers in the spring and summertime, having a cigarette, she'd said, thinking of Peterborough. The bungalow they'd been looking at was out on the edge. A very nice one – though the increase they'd seen in the value of their once-upon-a-time council house was offset by the decreases they had both seen in their fast-approaching pensions – and to a curiously exact level, once they had done the mathematics.

Now Miss Manjit Balrai was Access Development Manager for Strategy Solutions – Claire's thirty years of experience in the field counting for nothing after she'd tried to show Manjit the ropes and had simply been given the brush off. Manjit had studied Access Development, it turned out – to degree level – and had been awarded a 2:1.

His heart had gone out to Claire, watching as she was forced to relinquish leadership of the team. He knew how it felt to be superseded. For fifteen years, Stan had worked in the manufacture and sale of typewriters. Smith Corona had given him a 1921 beauty as a golden handshake in '94. It sat in the middle of his desk at home with its tiny round keys and long-dry ribbons – both red and black.

Though the house doesn't look the same now. Once a place of ordinary evenings, all the things Stanley's so familiar with have been painted dark. This morning, as twilight retreats, there's yellow tape across the front door.

In what was previously the living room, two walls are papered with nothing but grey flakes, falling, weightless in the light of a disclosing day. Silence lies flat on the floor. Footprints are everywhere.

'It's consistent,' the first had said, as they'd stood in the doorway with their report books.

'Maybe if the thing had been on standby. He was talking to one of the Holloway boys when they were still in here. He was watching it he told them.'

'Just after she'd died.'

'That's what he said.'

The television had stood somewhere in the corner. A slightly less damaged area of carpet highlights where the hospital bed had been and here beside it, in the centre of the room, a pile of lilac towels lies.

Stanley Parsons, sitting half a mile away, has discovered that he doesn't care what decisions they came to last night, or whether they find him or not. He's chosen only to care about non-cooperation – with everything – a white reaction – non-cooperation with the funeral or the police or with the choice between throwing and washing the towels.

Stanley's eyes are full of old pictures that he doesn't want anymore, but despite this he keeps expecting people to look at his face. They think he's homeless – they don't know the story. They don't understand that he could get up if he wanted now.

Bakeries are opening, and builders' cafés. Stan watches people arrive. They walk the pavement, appreciating the sunshine, and look both ways as they cross the road. He must speak to someone about food. The street smells of bacon, exhaust fumes and new daytime. Now the tube station is awake. He must have sat through an exceptional three hours outside Archway station. There's usually at least one mad person here.

Stanley realises that this man is mad before anything else, really before he even sees his face, because of the way he keeps looking into his carrier bag for encouragement, when there can't be anything in there that normal people would find reassuring. Stan can wait, talk to someone normal. But they probably won't know where to get food from. He has to talk to this man.

Stanley stands up as the first thin stream of Underground passengers surfaces and breaks around him. He's been completely on his own, he sees, just because he's been sitting on the ground.

This man is also sitting, in the first patch of sun, much further down Junction Road, holding a bottle of yoghurt drink and making syllables silently with his mouth. Approaching slowly, Stanley thinks he's mouthing gibberish but, looking over the man's shoulder at the ingredients list, it turns out he's being quite accurate.

Behind him, Stanley clears his throat. The man grabs his carrier bag and turns in one smooth movement to clutch it to himself. He takes a second to make sure that he has it, Stan sees – and in this moment realises something about the tramp's life very clearly, that he himself hasn't wholly recognised. He can't trust his own nerves and senses. If the world shrinks as you get madder then this person is very mad, because his world has become smaller than his body.

'I don't want your bag,' Stanley tells him, calmly and confidently, though in fact he doesn't know what's in it.

But Douglas Johnson only opens his mouth and shouts at Stan in the morning sunshine – maybe something else from the ingredients list.

Lowering his upraised hands and moving hastily away, Stan shudders, missing the transformation to undisguised curiosity that occurs across Douglas Johnson's face as soon as his back is turned.

Stan shudders.

He remembers once seeing a homeless person's toenails and being disgusted by how long they had grown, yellow as claws. But looking down at his own feet as he wanders away from the hobo seated behind him, he almost seems to be able to feel the nails grow – slowly but uncontrollably becoming disgusting.

He gazes around, remembering the moment that Les Dennis's face had started to sizzle. He watches a woman walk two dogs past his knees. A group of labourers push by on his other side. He says:

–

He used to have destinations.

He slows to a halt.

He could steal toenail clippers from the chemist's, but he doesn't want to steal, not even something so small and stupid. It occurs to him, if there's the Salvation Army where homeless people can shower, there must be a drop-in centre somewhere where they can have their fingernails clipped or hair cut. Where they can be kept in working order. Just one or two visits a month and they'd be able to prevent you from reverting. In some ways, his body is now his enemy.

The world turns around him and Stanley Donald Parsons wants to get off. He wants to go back to normality; he hasn't given it up voluntarily. He was never the sort of person who needed to take a stand. He and Claire hadn't even wanted a lot; they'd never expected to retire as millionaires. In the spectrum of the world's desires, really theirs had been on short leash. No one expects to die in agony at fifty one.

He could go back to his house and begin an attempt at reconstruction. Somewhere in the burnt out bathroom, behind the mirror with its arc of soot stain, he has a pair of toenail clippers. Somewhere in the ruined study downstairs his passport might still lie. He has an identity. He'd never realised effort was entailed in one before.

He stares at the Co op's wide doorway and the people moving there. Where are they moving to? He isn't going. What becomes of a person when they just stop?

The answer seems so simple, revelatory. You sit down on the pavement and there is nowhere lower. The answer seems as bright and blank and obvious as a flashing neon EXIT sign. A person stops and the world doesn't blink, but only continues to walk on.

Doug Johnson stands fifty yards from the bus stop and hails buses all day long every day but none of the buses ever stop for him there.

Once a man of letters, it was the conformity of children that had ruined Douglas's life. He'd first begun to consider retirement on the day that his form's debating team of thirteen years olds mustered a vote 'For' the use of school uniform. He'd sat misty-eyed and afflicted with a helpless smile as they'd nodded over the idea that uniforms helped prevent the bullying of those who would otherwise be wrongly clothed. It was the conformity of children – and of adults of course – which had left Douglas without vowels eventually. On the streets like this. A man of only one letter: G.

Now Douglas had loved children. He hadn't wanted to 'fuck' children, as they'd said. He'd wanted to bring generations into life who owned their own minds: proud young independent thinkers who might one day change the country. Had the whole fiasco not occurred, he most certainly would have retired. A career in teaching had left him hopeless. Insanity was the only reply that you could give the world.

Douglas *was* in some senses an anarchist. Throughout his life he had railed against the system – against enthrallment to the system – but in the end the system had won. It had caught him with an erection and a picture of a fifteen year old female pupil – and it had rooted him out; ejaculated him.

Now everyone likes girls in school uniform. This is a simple law of life – of the calibre, 'everyone likes food', or 'everyone likes sunsets'. A girl in school uniform is, for oft-unidentified reasons, attractive simply by the nature of her dress. Douglas had written an extensive and important essay however, *The Fetishisation Of Our Children* – and e-published it. Because there, deep in the aesthetic of those clean navy lines and white blouses, lies the nucleus of evil. He'd never said he was immune.

Yes, throughout life Doug had attempted to defy the system – in his later years the world around him had seemed a prison – but finally the system had shown its worth, discovering him within its midst and declaring him a monster.

Douglas Johnson's madness had begun with anger and had not ended yet.

The 91 goes by and Douglas Johnson screams obscenities; the passers-by widen their berth. He has an Oyster card – it isn't his – or he isn't Grace Killick – but as he holds it out before their oncoming flat red faces, he thinks to himself that the machines can't prove that.

It had occurred to Stan, in the year after he was made redundant, that he was useless. It had occurred to him that in the greater frame of history, say the evolution of mankind, he was a dead end. Had he been better equipped to anticipate the advent of the personal computer, would he have changed professions? The answer is no. He has always loved typewriters. He is innately, perhaps genetically, a cul-de-sac.

Claire at least made a dent on the world; left the access of Strategy Solutions' every client in a far more developed state than she found it. Whereas Stanley must look at his life – which finally found him acting as security guard for a great number of computers – and ask himself why.

Every place his eye turns to though, the question of why now seems to have risen to the surface. For instance, the advertisement for a Sony Minidisc Player that dominates the right-hand stretch of Junction Road. *Sarah*, it says. *Just recorded her first minidisc*. Then it gives the date. Sarah looks moved but emotionally grounded. Translucent grey light infuses her face and the room around her. Though a citizen of the real world, her expression suggests new vistas.

Claire never recorded a minidisc – not in her whole life. He thinks about vinyl and the way that vinyl gave way to tapes, how tapes surrendered to compact discs, which turned out not to be as compact as minidiscs, which are again very much larger than MP3s, that, as far as Stanley can make out, don't actually exist, because they're so small. Around him, piece by piece, every object is replaced by a smaller version of itself, until humans are giants, patrolling a Lego world.

Why? Stanley asks himself. Why? But the only answer that comes back to him is:

Why not?

At some indefinite point between the morning and the afternoon, a girl walks out of the lunchtime throng to where Stanley is sitting. She holds out her hand to him and in it is a Big Mac Meal bag – and it is full.

She says nothing. She has bits of metal in her face, her clothes are all black tights with holes and mini-skirts. She looks for dog butts while he eats her food – wandering away towards the junction – and though she turns and glances back as she reaches the roadside, stuttering a little with her steps, she does not come back.

Such an act of kindness looks pretty bright to Stanley, sitting beside the constant rev and crawl of traffic through Archway's centre, bereaved and unable to go home. He is disarmed already and, when she returns two hours later and, in the bustle, stops for a moment before him to say: 'Why not get drunk?' and then moves on again, he's very vulnerable. Although *Why not get drunk?* is not in itself a philosophical question, today, because he can find no answer, it hurts his soul. He watches her go and noiselessly reiterates the question. The words have their own taste.

If Claire is dead, he thinks, and the world he sees is godless, why not get drunk?

Claire Elizabeth Cartwright Parsons had gone for her first biopsy on the 14th of April. It would have been far earlier but, upon finally getting through to Newham Hospital after three weeks of unanswered calls, Stanley had found that they'd failed to make the appointment for the follow-up test for which she'd been told to wait. Speaking to a human being finally, Stanley had enquired when it *would* be possible and the receptionist had told him any day that week. In fact, three days later he and Claire received a small card informing them that her new appointment had been cancelled because actually Claire fell within the remit of The Whittington, on Highgate Hill, and not Newham Hospital at all, where she'd been rushed after her first collapse outside work.

When the test results came back from The Whittington – two months after the word 'biopsy' had first been used – Claire's throat cancer had metastasised and progressed to lymphoma, not confined to any particular remit at all.

Outside the foyer of The Whittington Hospital there's a stall that sells fruit. Grapes cost five pounds fifty a bunch there, but there's a market, you know, and if you'd never been into that car park then you hadn't yet been forced to understand that.

'That's life, mate, innit?' the man selling them would have said. And it is. And death too.

Stanley should be organising the funeral now. When the undertaker made a preparatory visit, he was given a brief description of the proper seating order for the hearses. There are guidelines. Society is the god of results.

Douglas Johnson sits touching his lower lip over and over again, speaking or maybe singing to himself. There's obviously a rhythm to it. Every so often a smile breaks gently across his face as his foot jiggles on and on.

His figure is a little twisted blip amidst the currents of pedestrians. What kind of madness is it that he has? Stan pictures the man's life: in and out of diagnosis, treatment, care, until the state can't afford him anymore.

Another possibility comes to mind now though: simple circumstances led Doug here and slowly he became like this.

This indeterminate insanity, then sleeping sickness in the end. You see them closing their eyes to the world, you see their faces swollen up against the world, lying on paving stone or on concrete or marble. Their sleep seems natural. Maybe Stan's always assumed that alcohol or cold nights are what leave these people drowning days in their own unconsciousness. Or that homelessness is like disease; it just leads to this kind of breakdown.

There are other countries though, where homelessness is a different thing – there are billions of refugees out there. Losing a grip on your home doesn't just cause you to lose a grip on yourself, surely?

Douglas likes to concentrate on G. Generally, things tend to stay within the confines of good while he goes on this way. G has always been his favourite letter. Its sound is soft and comforting. Or strong.

He likes to talk about things that begin with G – and there are so many. Government, gun control, genetics, God. You name it. At a point in his life, Douglas had a problem with parameters, but now that's gone.

He would tell Stan – though Stan might not listen – and he can't because it doesn't begin with G – life is too big for anyone. It must be filtered down. Focused. Though Douglas doesn't like the concept, the truth is, it's far more comfortable to be constrained.

Four o'clock traffic is starting to take hold and the thoroughfares of the city thicken. Shifts are changing; employees exchanged. Now the traffic lights revolve; everywhere Stanley looks, he sees the world catering for itself.

Is anyone looking for him? Maybe someone's getting it in the neck right now for letting him walk away. The fire brigade aren't the police though – perhaps it's not their responsibility. Yesterday one of the fighters told him – did he ask? – the brigade didn't *have* to hand their reports over to the police, unless they were sure a crime had been committed.

Do they search the streets, the homeless people, when suspects disappear?

There *has* to be a crime, of course, for there to be suspects. But there are such thin lines between crimes and non-crimes. He doesn't want to have to try and explain that to them.

It's like there has existed a pact between Stanley and

the world he sees. There must have been if one of them has broken it.

Outside the abandoned Abbey National, he sits in the progression of the afternoon. If he doesn't go back to talk to the police, he has no access to their accounts or to the social, nor even to a fresh change of clothes. He has no way to make a phone call. Everything will continue to be denied him. The right to grieve in private certainly, or the possibility of any future afterwards – the value in their home, in fact entitlement of any kind. Though he's worked all his life to consolidate the things he owns, one step from the path leaves him bereft.

It comes to him that the decision he faced in the living room last night was greater than it had first seemed. A towel in each hand and very few thoughts in his mind, he had failed to recognise how many things were provisional.

DAY # 2

Stanley has consumed one Big Mac Meal in twenty four hours; he needs more. Last night, as was recommended to him, he managed to get drunk. As the pubs had grown busier and the night sky darker, Stan had stood outside The Green Man and watched Bacchus rule. Men and women laughed over nothing, so loud that they muffled the juke box's cries. They'd leaned on each other as though in love and their pretty evening clothes had suffered slow subsidence.

Stanley's own clothes were not quite ruined yet. He'd finally moved through the smoke tight double doorway and sat quickly beside a dead halfpint. His tipple of choice had always been bitter, but the halfpint had been Carling. He'd drunk it with distaste. After ten minutes, moving tables, he'd had two unfinished vodka and cokes. The night had swarmed with warm drunkenness around him and Stanley had bottom-dived until, outside the empty Abbey National, he'd finally been able to pass out.

He was lucky in one way, he'd thought as he'd woken this morning. It was August and the pavement was already warm.

He can't remember the last time this building society branch was functional. It's red and grey stripes still adorn the wide windows and ten yards from him, above the grey-screened hole-in-the-wall, the sign still reads *Need Some Cash? Get It Here.*

Empty-pocketed though, an idea has come to Stan.

Last night, before the drinking had begun, before the Co-op had finally closed its smoothly sliding doors, he had watched two young Indian men roll out a green lidded skip and deposit into it two unmarked bags.

The supermarket has not yet reopened. For the second time, Stan has watched dawn bring slow life to the junction. It's beautiful; a quiet gathering that happens unbidden.

The skip still stands there. Just outside. It's five forty five am and if he's going to make a move it has to happen now, before the bin men come.

The tarmac is a dry streambed as Stanley looks both ways. He can hear the separate sounds of vehicles, distant and diverging. In the centre of the road, just for a moment, Stanley stops. No buses, no cars, no vans. Just one or two pedestrians. He looks down at the evenly broken white line that runs between his feet and imagines Claire driving past him on her way to work. Her thoughts would have been full of the day ahead (not this early of course, but not much later). She would have been smoking a Benson and listening to Terry Wogan on Radio Two. He doesn't have a radio or a cigarette. In the little pause that occupies Junction Road, standing motionless, he has no thoughts for the day before him. He pictures Claire's face as she spots him standing here, and pulls into the empty bus stop, winding down her window.

'What are you doing, Stan? For God's sake,' she'd say. She wouldn't recognise his expression: confusion, non-specific and un-rooted.

He imagines trying to explain it all to her: that just a few months of illness and one malfunctioning TV have done this to him. Even imagining, he feels shame.

He crosses the rest of the dead road and stands before the Co-op's skip. The lid is wet with dew and some brown stain but his hands are dirty anyway. With two glances over his shoulder, he lifts its wobbling weight and looks inside at the two black bags. Condensation has gathered in their folds.

Maybe they hold packaging and old till receipts. But the shapes that push the plastic out are rounded.

He looks around again, though no one's here to witness it. He's salivating as he tears a hole in the first bag.

Stanley smiles. For a moment he looks up at the sky, which is shrouded by morning cloud but might still break into sunlight. Under his hands, there are loaves of bread and bread rolls.

Turning again to the street he's just crossed, he looks for Douglas Johnson's ruined face but the tramp isn't here to call to. It's an amazing thing. It's a little blessing in a bin liner. All night, these rolls – pain rustique and wholemeal – have lain here covered, unbeknownst to everyone.

From far off, Stan hears the first sound of a lorry and without opening the second bag, pulls them both from their hideaway and trots back to the pavement by the cash machine with a breakfast that no one can prove isn't his.

In the few remaining areas of Docklands that have not already been transformed, large billboards display the things to come. In their pictures, computer generated office workers and home owners wander through computer generated tree-lined avenues and in and out of translucent doorways.

It was a wasteland before, this area. Now it is almost complete. You can already buy the last few flats that have not yet been built. *Own the Beauty*, the signs suggest, on the walls that hide the empty sites. Claire might have, if she'd been able to afford it before dying. She'd always wanted a river view.

Stanley remembers when he started work out there. He'd often found himself staring absentmindedly at this billboard, placed conveniently across the road and in the centre of his little window.

Own the Beauty.

The people are small and their world is very large, but they look happy and the sun is shining, nuclear war is not a threat to them. Certainly they will never need to have pink mush pumped into their rotting stomachs in order to live a few days longer. They will simply disappear as soon as their mortgages are paid.

He had heard someone say – maybe Pete, maybe Lol – that there was only one computer in the building where he'd been contracted, four day-shifts and one nightshift per week, even though there were so many different machines. He remembers shrugging. The truth is, he doesn't really know what any of those machines did. Or *do* – because obviously the place doesn't disappear just because he stops turning up to work. He wonders if that's what the office in the *Own the Beauty* sign would do.

Stan still has a week before he's supposed to return to

work. The funeral should be approaching. But he doesn't imagine that there's much left of Claire for them to bury, judging by the way their home had burned. Wallpaper is highly flammable – they don't tell you that in Habitat. Armchairs are kindling, upholstered.

Who takes care of her funeral now that he's gone? Will it happen automatically?

He wants there to be a funeral. But he won't go back and explain to them every detail of her death – and justify himself – to earn one for her. It's wrong to die without a memorial, but what they're asking from him is worse.

Besides, he can't prove anything.

Stanley sits with the two black bags between his open legs. His trousers, which were once part of a suit from Marks and Sparks, have developed large discoloured patches round the ankles. He remembers Claire ironing them with *Coronation Street* on. It was never some perfect moment, not while it was happening, but looking back on it, it has a sepia tone. They were lucky to be ironing and watching telly, he realises. They were lucky not to be dead.

In the second black bag, Stanley has found himself twenty five rhubarb flavoured Müller Corners. They won't even pass their use-by date until tomorrow. They taste delicious and their texture is like heaven in little vacuum-formed plastic squares. With both the bread and the yoghurt in his hands, he almost feels like he's scored points against the world. To think, if he hadn't crossed the road, these things might have been loaded into the rubbish truck and driven away from him.

Douglas makes his entrance at 10 a.m. today. Emerging from Bickerton Road into the high street, he levels his gaze on the task ahead. He'll take his place, exactly halfway between this first bus stop and the next (near to which, Stanley sits) and he will raise his arm at each approaching routemaster and bendybus – and perhaps today one driver will stop for him. Eventually, it will happen. Time is on his side.

His aims have narrowed over the last few years. Where once he had fantasised about schooling a generation to open their minds and, in their later years, move into local government, the voluntary sector, into teaching themselves, or maybe even anarchism, now he concentrates his efforts in a single stream.

Eventually, a driver will stop for him right here.

He understands the necessity of structure: deep down, where sadness lies underneath all the anger he's collected, he knows that the system is not inflicted, but that it rises like spring water, inside everyone, to create this world, which suits us best. But he can't rid himself of the dissident urges that have plagued him since he was eight years old.

Douglas used to dream of revolution but it never would have done him any good. Throughout his whole life – in fact, since the very first time his father dressed him in a girl's school uniform and locked him in the cupboard under the stairs – this war has filled Douglas's heart; he can't escape from it.

Betty was the name of the girl who overthrew him. Betty Pullman. She gave him the photograph. He would never have asked for it from her.

Having made his way to his workplace, Doug stands, gazing on towards the Abbey National, looking at Stan and his black plastic bags. There are people moving between them now and his view is intermittent: eating, then nothing, then Stan's hands inside the bags.

Doug's never late for work.

Today, he thinks, he can spare ten minutes.

With his own carrier bag clasped in both hands, he makes his way towards Stan's figure and begins to compose his words.

Stanley raises his head. Though when he discovered the food, he'd actually looked around for Doug, now he's begun to eat it, he finds his hands tightening around the plastic bags – just as Doug's did yesterday. Amidst the sounds of the traffic and the footsteps, he examines the tramp's features but can't make out his motives through the strange expression that precedes Doug's first words.

'Government,' Doug says.

'What?'

But Doug doesn't answer. He begins to rearrange his clothing and before Stan can speak, he is sitting down beside him and has his own hands in Stan's black plastic bread bag. He doesn't stop the tramp, but he feels a kick of anger – of selfishness, he supposes.

'Government,' Doug continues, with a bread roll in one hand, 'comprises the set of legal and political institutions that regulate the relationships amongst members of the society and between the society and outsiders.'

His face has settled – into some form of arrogance, Stanley thinks, or tutorial pride.

The tramp's clothes are multi-layered: shirts and jumpers and a yellow body warmer underneath a dog-tooth check coat. He is wearing flip-flops and his filthy toes wriggle at the ends of his splayed legs.

'These institutions have the authority to make decisions for the society– ' he stops. Stan watches him take a breath, as if this pause was intended. ' –policies affecting the maintenance of order and the achievement of certain societal goals. The citizen, in effect, surrenders a certain amount of individual sovereignty to the government in return for the protection of life and property and the provision of essential services.'

For a few passing instants, the strangeness of the situation escapes Stan and he hears the meaning of the words.

'Did you make that up?'

Seemingly finished with his lecture, Doug begins to eat bread. His own carrier bag lies, protected, half-inside the folds of his coat. His face is bearded and dark-lined and the whites of his eyes have a yellow tinge.

He eats with his mouth open, wet bread passing in and out of sight, sparing a glance for the second, more closely-guarded Muller Corner bag.

'My name's Stan,' Stan says quietly after a moment or two. 'Stanley Parsons.'

'I'm Douglas Johnson,' the tramp answers, as if he's sane.

'What was that…? That you were saying?'

Raising one finger, Doug taps it against his nose. 'G,' he says knowingly.

It's peaceful, sitting here. Though around them, there is a great deal of activity and people speak with agitation into their mobile phones, right here on the pavement, there's little to worry about. A man is sweeping the other side of the road. The Co-op have a special on BEER + BREAD.

Because it's generally agreed that murder is unhelpful to the running of a stable society, or perhaps because there's always been such a lot of financial potential in the business of protecting people, it's important that the truth about what happened in Stanley's living room is discovered and recorded – that all necessary retribution is meted out. Someone has this duty. Perhaps several someones. This very moment, they must be hard at work.

Stan doesn't know them. The whole idea leaves him with a sense of wonder. He and Douglas sit with their backs against the wall. They're surrounded by men and women going about their daily lives, necessary people, of which he is no longer one. From here, the world is nothing but a view. He's never noticed the efficiency before. A race that spawns a person for every task. What if no one wanted to be a policeman, he wonders. Or what if everyone wanted to be a policeman but there wasn't any crime? It must be part of the beauty of nature that neither of these situations has occurred.

'It's amazing, isn't it?' he says quietly, because he'd rather speak to Douglas than to no one. 'It's amazing, how everything works. You put a plug in a socket and you flick a switch. You get up in the morning and you go to work. Everyone's so confident.' He sees their shoes and legs go by. 'It's amazing.'

'Goethe,' Douglas says, as his fingers reach like insects towards Stanley's second black bag. 'Generally recognised as one of the greatest and most versatile European writers and thinkers of modern times, Johann Wolfgang von Goethe, born August 28th 1749, profoundly influenced the growth of literary ROMANTICISM.'

Stan watches him. He's obviously mad. And yet, in some ways, there doesn't seem to be much wrong with him. Eventually Stan passes him a Muller Corner, for which Douglas does not thank him.

'Goethe himself expected to be remembered as a scientist,' Doug says, as he works his fingers around the little flap of peel-back foil. 'Biology has long recognised its debt to him, especially for the concept of morphology, which is fundamental to the theory of evolution. As determinism ceases to characterize science, it is finding a greater tolerance for a Goethean world in which all phenomena tend to merge.' With a satisfied smile, Doug removes the foil cover and licks it clean. Turning to Stanley and handing it back to him, striped by tongue-marks, he finishes with a flourish, *'There is nothing in living nature which is not in relation to the whole.'*

But if that's the case, Stan thinks, as the buses trundle past them, then why are they both here?

For a while after September the 11th – and to a lesser extent the 7/7 bombings – it had felt as if the world might be ending, but now everyone seems fairly sure that that's not the case. Stan remembers both events very clearly, as everybody in the universe must. He'd listened

38

to the 7/7 bombing reports on the radio, a useful running commentary on the chaos. The names of underground stations had flown to join the list of battlegrounds and journalists had had to run to keep up. *It's in Kings Cross! It's in Old Street! It's in Hackney!* On the Holly Lodge Estate, outside Stanley and Claire's kitchen window, a council worker with a Flymo had continued to cut the grass, while on *Capital*, gasping survivors were interviewed.

Stan had watched the man. Recovering from his weekly nightshift, Claire had been at Strategy Solutions and his cup of tea had been slowly growing colder on the table in front of him. He'd wondered if the council worker had no radio – or if the order had already come to him, to keep on mowing. And as it turned out the man had been right. The world hadn't ended and his work had been as necessary as ever.

'What's in your bag, Doug?' Stanley asks.

But the tramp looks up at him as if he's just been threatened. He takes a last dashing glance at the yoghurts, gathers his clothes, his carrier bag, and flees.

It's no wonder the man's homeless, Stan thinks, with an attitude problem like that.

For a few moments, he considers standing and taking the five minute walk home. He doesn't want to end up spouting gibberish at people's simple questions, or guarding a carrier bag as though it holds his life and soul.

A slow chain of probabilities plays itself through Stanley's mind. He returns to their council house and tries to rejoin preparations for Claire's funeral. He tries to use the phone but it's melted and no longer functioning. He tries to find the clothes in which her burnt corpse should be buried but finds that they have also been destroyed. And at some point, he encounters the authorities – for this is something he cannot avoid – and then he's faced with finding answers again.

He can't prove he didn't kill Claire. 'It was an act of God,' he imagines telling them.

But such things can't be used as a reasonable defence anymore.

There must be a million reasons for ending up on the streets, Stan thinks, as he sees Douglas sit on a bench a hundred yards away. But maybe when you break them down they're really all the same. No matter how tough life gets, you can't stop going along with it.

On the 21st of March, which had been a Thursday, Claire had been booked for the creation of her mask. This had been essential before the treatment could progress. Her 'mask' was a personally-fitted protective shield, which she would wear during her radiotherapy sessions but not at any other time.

They had parked as per usual outside St Bartholomew's – Claire's third and final hospital. Farringdon had been miserable under the spring.

They hadn't seen the sign. With total and complete honesty, Stanley was capable of saying that they had not seen the sign. Nonetheless, the assigned hospital parking bay had not been functional, and the sign – as they were later shown – had clearly been displayed. Despite the fact that they had often parked in just the same spot before, on the 21st of March, when they had gone down for her cigarettes between fittings, they'd discovered that they'd been given a forty pound fine. The inspector wasn't able to tell her why the bay had become non-operational.

The next day, amazingly, the same thing had happened in just the same way but with the adjacent bay. Once again they were fined. Claire had suffered a breakdown at that point and needed to go home. She'd wanted to finish the fitting, obviously, because she had wanted to submit her body to the radiotherapy as soon as possible and kill the cancer that had been killing her. That Thursday afternoon however, she'd been incapable of doing more than sobbing as Stan had held her hand. That night, Stan had sat down to write to Ken Livingstone but had got no further than putting down his name.

On the pavement, he now sings a song to himself. He remembers all the flowers that had come in those final weeks, their living room transformed by them. Cards had graced every inch of the mantelpiece and, between the new pieces of equipment that had come to rule their lives, lilies had sprouted from vases, disguising cables, hiding plastic tubes. He'll never enjoy the smell of lilies again. He knows them now for what they really are.

He will never again buy a towel set. Where before he'd always enjoyed the colour coordination of their little rounded stack against the bathroom wall, now he has first-hand knowledge of that which the soft furnishing manufacturers seek to hide: towels were not invented as decorative objects, but as absorbent rags.

It is this, as much as the call for explanations, which prevents him from ever going home. How can death make everything seem useless, when it goes on every moment of every day? Stanley imagines making a sign and holding it while he sits here. But he doesn't know how he'll reduce all this confusion into one single question, let alone an answer, let alone 'the truth'.

Lol had liked to look at porn during his shifts, out of preference the readers' wives. He'd used to read out little snippets to Stanley, like 'randy wet grandma wants you to pump her hard.' Glancing over Lol's shoulder, Stan had often marvelled aloud at how such material came to exist, or be in common circulation. As if chastised, Lol had said in the voice that he reserved solely for excusing himself, 'Well, there's a market, you know...'

But everything can be explained this way, like pop-tarts and TV shows that humiliate people for fun, and depleted uranium shells, and journalism, and mineral water with a hint of peach. He's very thirsty after all that bread and yoghurt.

At about midday, with the desire for water occupying most of Stanley's thoughts, he attempts to go into The Green Man again. Since leaving his house two nights before, he hasn't emptied his bowels and the combined appeal of a tap and a toilet has grown too strong.

He chooses to wait and enter on the heels of a couple who must have money and can legitimately walk inside, but as he begins to follow them through the door, the woman turns and clutches her handbag and asks him in an outraged voice what he is doing. At that point the bartender crosses the pub, ushers the couple inside and stands in front of Stan with folded arms.

'You can't come in here, mate,' he says.

'I wasn't trying to steal from her.'

'Whatever,' the bartender replies.

'Can I use your toilet?' Stanley asks him. And he does see a flicker of sympathy, but the man says:

'Mate, it's more than my job's worth.'

Stanley isn't really sure what that means. The man can't be more than twenty six or twenty seven but there isn't an ounce of respect in his face. This is not a change that's happened overnight though. For quite a few years now, Stan's noticed that whatever it takes to earn respect from the young – money or power or a decent MP3 player – he doesn't possess.

'Can I have some water then?'

'If I go and get you water, you're just going to try and come inside. I'll have to push you out. It'll all get very messy. You don't want that.'

'No I don't,' Stanley says.

'So let's just leave it.'

'I won't try to come in.' He takes three steps backwards, until he's in the way of everyone on the pavement. 'See?' he says. 'Just a glass of water.'

'Alright,' the bartender wipes at his eyes with exhaustion, 'but just don't try to come inside.' He turns back to Stan as he reaches the bar. 'Ice and lemon?' he asks.

At about quarter past one a really funny thing happens. A man in a suit passes Stan, who's sitting by the Abbey National once again, and he reaches into his pocket to pull out a ten pound note.

He hands it to Stanley with the words, 'Why not get drunk?'

No matter how you look at it, *Why not get drunk?* is never a philosophical question. Yet sitting there with the beautiful, beige-coloured piece of paper in one hand, Stanley realises that now the usual constraints of work and time have left him, it requires a philosophical answer – which is something else that he does not possess.

The logic of buying ten bottles of Volvic (or twenty bottles of Turkish mineral water) is insufficient to prevent him. Even the appeal of

Pizza. On a Roll.

Though he's hungry and will grow hungrier, what Stan's really missing is company and he rightly assumes that a bottle of Bells will buy him that.

If the world is nothing more than a giant lump of rock, wheeling mindlessly through the universe's physical laws, creating life without reason, why not get drunk?

Hannah comes out every day to pick up cigarette butts – and the bus stop beside which Stan has made his new home is always her best hunting ground. Here people light and discard them without even caring. Hannah isn't homeless, she's a squatter; though there are walls between the place where she sleeps and the outside world, they are not walls that belong to her. She doesn't believe in ownership. She doesn't believe in borders, or love, or sobriety. She's in search of oblivion, but so far it's proved quite hard to find.

Hannah wears a little badge on her collar, which reads

Fuck You And Your Last Rolo

As she stands looking down at Stan, he reads it several times. He recalls the advertising campaign and he doesn't know how to respond to her, after yesterday's combination of generosity and venom. Today she holds no food. It's his turn to give.

'Well... this looks cosy...' she says. She points at the bottles of Bells and Cola that stand next to him, just opened, then asks politely, 'Can I join you?'

Her English is good but her accent is foreign – Stanley can't make out where from.

'Please do,' he says.

She sits without elegance – her chewed tights baring legs that show hair, her belts clinking. She has a pretty face, without make up, and bad skin.

'It's lovely isn't it?' she says. 'Just to sit. It's so relaxing. I like to relax.'

'I haven't got any cups,' Stanley tells her.

'We can drink a little from this one and little from that one.'

'Yes ok.' After a moment, he picks up the whisky and offers it to her.

'Muchos gracias.'

'Are you Spanish?'

She drinks heavily and exhales the fumes with a long, slow breath.

'No.'

'But you're not from here.'

'I'm from *everywhere*...' She passes the bottle back. 'Grazi tanto. Efharisto. Baie dankie. Thank you very very much.'

But Stan just holds it. It must all seem very sordid, he thinks, to the people walking past. But when he glances up to see the faces, no one's even looking at them. He's no longer sure what Claire would make of this.

The whisky tastes revolting but it makes Hannah smile at him.

'I haven't seen you around here very much before. Are you in a hostel?'

'No,' he says.

'Squatting?'

'No.'

'I always squat. So you're sleeping here.'

'I slept here last night.'

'Nice.' She drinks again. 'Well it's going to get busy now. Things will start to come out of the walls now it's the weekend... all the crawly people.'

'What day is it?'

'Friday,' she says.

He doesn't answer, absorbing this information, trying to remember which day it was when Claire died. Wednesday. Tuesday. He's not sure, which leaves him with a sense of apprehension.

'I'm Hannah,' she goes on, fishing for something in his expression.

'Stanley Parsons.'

'Stanley Parsons.' She nods. 'So you know how everything works?'

'What?'

'Things.' She gestures to the phone box. 'Usual things...'

But she can't be asking him how a telephone works.

She examines his obvious uncertainty and then she says, 'You want brown?'

'What?'

'Brown, Stanley.'

But the colour is a mystery to him.

'You want a bag, ten pounds? You have ten pounds, no?' Her appraisal is very quick but she seems sure. And then Stan realises. She's talking about heroin. And for a brief instant, he feels a little frisson of excitement, to be having such a conversation at all. It's very brief though. He sees her skin again – spotted and transparent in the August light – and her long, inappropriate sleeves.

'If you have five, we can share,' she says seditiously.

The phone box that stands ten feet from him is the place from which the calls are made. Inside, sellotaped next to the slot that takes the money, a little scrap of paper bears a mobile number and no name.

This mobile number will only answer calls that come from this telephone box. The voice will say nothing except, 'How much? A tenner?' Then if you stand here, a man will come to you.

Stanley has sat beside the phone box for forty eight hours now, but has noticed none of this.

'You like brown?' Hannah asks him, looking again at him; at the cut of his trousers as he sits, legs outstretched.

He considers telling her that he's never tried it. He considers telling her that he's only ever smoked marijuana a couple of times in his life and both of them made him feel ill. But in the end, he mentions neither of these things.

'Not right now,' he says. But then he can't resist his curiosity. 'Do you like it?'

'I like everything,' she says, smiling misanthropically. 'Look.'

Picking through the many pockets and crannies of her multiple belts, the girl finally draws out a piece of paper. It is a brightly coloured fold-out leaflet and on its cover, in a sunlit autumn day, a woman and a young girl child wander through what looks like New Hampshire – to Stanley, who's never seen the USA. There are houses with verandas and well-tended meadows and the message:

Life in a Peaceful
New World

Stanley takes it from her and looks more closely.

The child is gently stroking the head of a playful grizzly bear. Turning it over, he follows the picture's continuation until he beholds a scene of pastoral tranquillity: a boy gathering apples and laughing. An African couple, who seem quite happy too. And in the background, what appears to be an Iranian family

48

playing with a lion. The father is holding his young daughter up so she can pat its head.

Opening the leaflet, Stanley reads, as Hannah continues to drink his Bells.

When you look at the scene on this tract,
what feelings do you have?
Does not your heart yearn for the peace, happiness,
and prosperity seen there? Surely it does.
But is it just a dream, or fantasy, to believe these
conditions will ever exist on earth?

'They gave it to me yesterday,' Hannah says.

'Who?'

'Jehovah's Witnesses, look.' And at the very end of the last page, in small print at the bottom, it does say Would you welcome more information? Write to Jehovah's Witnesses at the appropriate address below.

'Why Jesus?' she says. 'Try heroin.'

He'd once heard that the name Hannah meant grace. He remembers this now.

'...Or anything. Butane. Superglue. Nutmeg, it all works.' She looks towards the road and lines up another bent cigarette butt.

Stanley gazes from her young but pitted face down to the paper. He wonders if the people who'll live *in a Peaceful* **New World** will still have to pay council tax. He imagines the Iranian family laughing joyfully as they eat a full breakfast and open their bills. He imagines those little letters, with their green candy-striped edgings, which had continued to arrive throughout Claire's illness

49

as both their incomes had fallen away, now floating down through their soot-covered letterbox to lie on a burnt-out lino floor.

He asks for the bottle from Hannah again and watches the pedestrians flow past them. He has a realisation: he doesn't need to care.

'Nutmeg?' he asks her. 'Is that true?'

'I knew someone who ate half a jar. They woke up by the side of the road. Didn't have a memory of anything and it was three days later.'

Stan becomes conscious of the fact that he's tipsy. He examines Hannah's passive eyes as she smokes and thinks about the affordability of superglue.

A home is a wonderful thing. You feel safe when you're inside one; pretty much everything you're going to need is in a drawer. It's a necessity, if you're going to go to work, which is a necessity if you're going to pay your *Council Tax*. But it strikes Stan that this is a circle. *A Mobius life*. At no point in all the worrying and juggling of money that had outlined Claire's slow decline, at no point, on the phone to the bank, the credit cards, or during the making of any payment plan, had he stopped to examine the real consequences of irresponsibility. Non-payment of debts had always left him with such a great fear that he'd been unable to see exactly what he was afraid of. Sitting here, suddenly he sees: walk out of the house and close the door – and never go back – and there's nothing they can do.

'So what are you doing here, Stanley Parsons?' Hannah asks him, as if she has heard these thoughts.

'My house burnt down,' he says. 'Everything.' And

then he finds himself adding, 'I could go back.' But the ring of the words isn't truthful. Something irreparable has occurred.

It's ambition that keeps the world running – and maybe all of it is held in that gene they isolated and found a name for yesterday. But if that's the case, then that gene must be in *everything* – in dogs and grass and spiders. Ambition is the drive that gives life. Dogs and spiders and grass are unaware of the fact that life will leave them eventually, whatever they manage to achieve. But humans know this, Stan thinks. They just ignore it and get on with their days.

You can't ignore death when it's lying between your sofa and your sideboard on a hospital bed, occupying what's left of your wife. Maybe that's why palliative care in hospital is so popular. It's much more likely your ambition will continue if there's someone else to nurse your dying loved one. Death seems cleaner if a person in a uniform is there to manage it. Not as much of a spanner in the works. And this is the deal, Stan supposes. A little bit of ambition in each of us, neatly targeted toward our separate goals, and together we make a creation that cannot falter. Nurses nurse, security guards guard, a giant skills-bank forms itself and benefits each individual. And if your contribution happens to be in a field that evolution devalues and discards – typewriters for instance – then you must just look around and see the whole, which has taken your contribution, and continues to run smoothly in your wake. Continues moving forward. Progressing.

'Goethe,' Stan says quietly.

51

'What?'

'There is nothing in living nature which is not in relation to the whole.' But what exactly was the whole progressing towards? He watches the girl regretfully crush out the second cigarette butt and remembers Claire's full ashtrays. 'What's the point, do you think?' he asks Hannah. 'What's the point of life?'

She sticks her tongue out flat into the city's summer air and then withdraws it.

'The taste buds,' she answers unconditionally.

Claire had loved Sunny Delight. Where other brands of orange juice had often upset her stomach with high acid levels, Sunny Delight was far more gentle and she'd been able to accompany her breakfast with it every morning and never need a Zantac or a Rennie. Not only that, but they'd managed to design Sunny Delight in such a way as to instil it with a higher vitamin content than that of a real orange. It was incredible what people could achieve if there was a market.

In general, Claire had been a great connoisseur of new commodities – every month she'd had the *Innovations* catalogue delivered to their doorstep. Particularly partial to new cleaning products, every room in their house had been equipped with Neutra Air Freshmatic. In fact, even before Claire's illness, her life had been augmented with a range of helpful health-related goods. Natravene had kept her regular; at precisely five forty five every morning, she used to make her way to loo. HRT had allowed her to stave off the menopause. Aquaban, then later Aquaban Herbal had relieved her pre menstrual water retention and every day a small bottle of Yakult had topped up her levels of good bacteria. Claire had liked to take care of herself and her home. Cancer targeted the most surprising people.

Stan remembers how the medical paraphernalia had begun to intersperse itself between these other products. The many pills, the charts, the special protein drinks, a wealth of tools to ascertain the levels at which her body was functioning, or failing to. But none of them had helped. The tubes had pumped in food and water, with their little machine breathing constantly under the TV's voice. The Neutra Air Freshmatic had continued to puff perfume into the room, but not at a sufficient rate to counteract the smells of sickness. In the end, Claire had slipped towards death while all of that equipment had lived on.

If the television hadn't exploded, he'd be picking up these things now and throwing them into the bin, or returning those on hire to St Bartholomew's. He pictures himself pressing the wastebasket pedal over and over, delivering each pharmacological packet to its final resting place – complete with its instructions stapled to the side.

Recalling the moment when he'd looked up at the TV screen and seen Les Dennis's face sliding in multicoloured pixels down towards the volume and contrast controls, Stanley thinks to himself, God moves in mysterious ways.

Stanley reads the leaflet carefully as he and Hannah grow drunker. It says:

There will be every reason to be happy in the Paradise earth. Never again will people hunger for lack of food. "They will certainly plant vineyards and eat their fruitage... they will not plant and someone else do the eating."

In God's new world, no longer will people be crammed into huge apartment buildings or run-down slums, for God has purposed: "They will certainly build houses and have the occupancy. They will not build and someone else have the occupancy. They will not toil for nothing."

Just imagine, in the Paradise earth all sicknesses will be healed! "God will wipe out every tear from their eyes, and death will be no more, neither will mourning nor outcry nor pain be anymore. The former things have passed away."

Towards the end of what they were later to see as her life, Stanley had noticed a growing disillusionment in Claire. Not something she would talk about easily, access development had begun to raise questions, moral questions – and like many moral questions, they kept arising after the fact.

What if the company whose access you are developing produces something to which you don't believe anyone ought to have access?

It wasn't that Claire had liked censorship or that she'd wanted to live under a nanny state, but the full-throttle logic of 'there's a market, you know...' must have seemed to pale as an excuse with passing time. When

Claire had returned home one evening – not too long before her illness had begun – and sat before her desktop with her logistics spreadsheets open and one hand covering her mouth in what had looked like doubt, Stan had asked her what the matter was. And turning to him, her expression worn and unfamiliar, she'd said:

'Client confidentiality, Stan, you know I'm not allowed to say.'

Her computer screen had hummed a gentle, pixilated blue.

'Don't give me any details,' he'd said. 'Just talk in general terms.'

'Do you think access development is a good thing?'

'What, ethically?'

'Ethically.'

'Well it depends, I suppose…'

'On what?'

He'd shrugged. 'On whether it does people good…?'

'Yes, but sometimes,' she'd answered, 'it's just too hard to tell. I mean sometimes you can't trace the consequences.'

'Look, if it was that bad,' Stan had told her with assurance, 'they would have made a law against it.'

After a moment of staring at the Excel window once again, all those small blank boxes waiting for her input, undiscriminating, Claire had asked, 'How would I know when to turn a client down?'

He'd raised his open palms and looked back at her without an answer.

Of course, the reality of the situation had been that Stanley wasn't really sure what 'access development' entailed. Even after twenty five years, when people asked him what his wife did for a living, he had found himself using words which had no sure substance, like 'analyst' or 'consultant'. Now he thinks about her job description from a broader perspective. Sitting here, he thinks that in some way the whole world's engaged in the process of access development. Wherever he looks, he can see no dead ends, except in the lives of the people themselves.

Typewriters had led to computers, hadn't they? And computers were almost bound to lead on further – to mobile phones with the capabilities of massive servers, or entire databases that were contained in one earring, or a semi colon that held the meaning of the world. Though he still doesn't know the specifics of Claire's reservations that night she'd sat in front of her PC, what grows clearer to Stan is the borderless sense of unease he'd seen in her. Surely progress isn't an end in itself.

Stan's second day slowly leans into an evening as he sits, pissed out of his head, on Junction Road. The sun shares its last light as the people stop working and begin to fill their hours with fun. In every street in the city, shutters are falling. Alarms are set, tills are cashed up and shop floors mopped clean. Everybody knows that this is Friday – including Stanley now.

On every side of him, for miles and miles, London continues to exist. Twilight is coming in Mill Hill – over tux n tails and Greenspans, over Eurodrive and Oriental Rugs Direct. The fading sky is infused with pinks that blend into the dust over Hackney and Harringey and Hornsey. People see their own faces in the windows of Al Bahia, Nethost Telecommunication and Flight Express

Travel. Anticipation of the coming weekend fills footsteps and voices. DH Lumsden's and JADE Entertainment and the Richard Adams Hair Salon cast graceful shadows across their paving stones. Even the traffic sounds different. There are radios playing. Pigeons take flight from the roof of Bobe Minicabs and circle in genome spirals above The Diamond School of Motoring. In Hendon and Neasden and Balham and Clapham and Streatham and Battersea and indeed Brent Cross, an hour comes – or thirty minutes – of magic, during which the sun and the streetlamps perform their exchange.

In the north, beside the multiple carriageways that siphon London's vehicles towards the rest of the UK, the TRIPLEPRINT DOUBLEPRINT BONUSPRINT sign reaches up, untouched by wind, a regal sunset refracted in its plastic. All in all, it's a beautiful evening. You can't help but marvel. Stan cries for a little while, because Claire can't see these things. But it is amazing, he thinks, nonetheless.

The Fully Licensed Gresham Hotel, the Power Tool Centre, Blue Lagoon, Advance Cash Register Limited, Glotech Computers, Xtra Staff, the Baba Gurgur Restaurant, Primo Pizza, Pizza Bono, Ready Pizza, Clarke Associates and Maccy D'S, The Brent Crescent Vehicle Pound, Leatherworld, Advance Business Telephone Systems and Ace Café London and Capitol Printing and Tesco and Dicey Reilly's Nightclub and Collect and Connect and Racenews and The Housing Association, and Stereovision, Kelvin Motor Wagons, the Cut & Style Barbers, Gilberts For BMWs and LoftRooms and Perspective Signs and the Davis and Davis Estate Agents.

It is amazing, to be surrounded by it all.

DAY # 2 (Night)

Watching the Docklands form itself with cranes and plate glass around him over the course of the last five years, Stan had sat before his bank of CCTV monitors and shaken his head at the expense of it all. The buildings had slowly coalesced round rising steel towers, which probed the skyline at an appropriate distance below that of Canary Wharf's maternal peak. But he'd reserved judgement, as some hadn't. After all, if a business chose to construct itself a headquarters, what moral position could he really take? It was their money to spend – and employment grew round these new buildings, in fact far better than the grass. Presumably at some point in the past, the founders of these businesses – for instance the banks – had made a sound investment, with money of their own, and had recouped it. How could one pass judgement on that? In Africa maybe, when mining had been all the rage, perhaps the original George Frederick Citibank had spotted an important niche market for harness equipment and lent a fiver to the local leathersmith. It was just that these days, with the many pinnacles of Natwest and Barclays and the HSBC ornamenting every dusk, it was hard for people to make out the root of it all.

The name of Stanley's employer had been Ellipse Systems; its little logo had accented the right hand corner of every monitor. Stanley's views had alternated on a relaxing rhythmical cycle; first inside then outside the Ellipse Systems building, where construction workers had mingled with the office workers already stationed in East 14. The numbers of those who inhabited the Docklands' working week had climbed, slow but steady, in Stanley's five years there: for every twenty be suited people that passed the security cameras, one might, for each day, add another. Imperceptible but important, like the sea level there on the other side of the Thames Barrier, remote and beautiful on the river's glassy shine.

It had been obvious that Ellipse Systems was not missing out on the general upsurge of wealth which was occurring. Here, the numbers of staff and machines also multiplied and there was talk – as there's always talk, whispers trickling down from high above – of a takeover bid. Pyramid Systems hadn't yet replaced the missing letters in their fascia, five hundred yards further down the Westferry Road, and it was clear to all and sundry that the fountain before their main entrance had remained unpolished throughout the entire summer. Though why one company should be enjoying such patent success while the other rotted was, at first, a mystery to Stan. He'd used to while away the odd fifteen minutes trying to superimpose the image of a pyramid onto the logo which he saw repeated at ten inch intervals on Ellipse's monitors, on every side. However he positioned the shapes though, he couldn't imagine anything that didn't look like a witch's hat.

The fax machine had often churned and hatched on the little desk behind him, the days or the evenings or nights had been softened by the ever-changing LED patterns on the servers that occupied his screens, and

Stan had found that the role of security guard was really based around the struggle of how to spend one's time. Pete and Lol had liked to replay videos – into tedium – of the few drunken brawls or shameless up-against-the-walls that had happened on their shifts. But Stan had really tried to do his job well. He'd watched the screens – and guarded – and watched them – and guarded. He hadn't wanted his employment to be superfluous.

For this reason only did he happen to see, issuing from the mute sister-fax machine that was pictured in black and white on the fifth monitor from the left (in a rotation of every three minutes), a single long communiqué, emerging strip by strip, that bore the unmistakable insignia of Strategy Solutions.

At home now, his wife's PC must be a stained and pale grey face amidst the blackened ornaments. It's easy, Stan thinks, to forget the power of simple things, maybe because everyone's so impressed with the complex ones. For a long time, he'd believed that they were in some way safe – as though it wasn't possible for the decoration of their lives to hang on unsound walls. But a well put-together library and several sets of matching candlesticks, a high no-claims bonus and a weekly delivery from Ocado were not forms of protection really, they just made your home seem more permanent. Fire and death, Stan thinks, fire and death, as he watches the Co-op's doors slide open and issue its customers back onto the street. They heft their carrier bags into more comfortable positions and walk away into the beginning of their night. The Qasar building's entrance opposite is dark and empty, as always, but the kebab shops are bright enough to light the sky. More slowly now, and with illuminated passengers, the buses pass Stan by.

The 41. The 134.

There's the odd timing fluctuation but it seems very regular. Just as it did at work, his view changes and repeats itself, but Stanley's not guarding anymore. It's Friday night now and he hasn't emptied his bowels for two days. He doesn't know any of the people who are beginning to advance into this territory. In Archway, on the Holloway Road and in Finsbury Park, money circles on tight reins at night. Fewer hands want fewer things. And Stan feels a little like he's fallen through a hole in their living room carpet and onto the other side of the world. Nothing that lies around like he's lying now is protected.

He tells himself that, although the Fire Brigade and the police – and the no-claims-bonus and the matching candlesticks – had seemed like pieces of a safe haven, in fact nothing of theirs had been sheltered. Cancer had come and emptied their lives. In the end, their possessions had burned while the emergency services had minimised disruption.

Of course, if he had stayed, and managed to absolve himself in the matter of Claire's helpless death, he might have been able to reap the protective benefits of their home insurance. From this he could have built another home – and hung another little set of key-hooks on the wall – but now, with all things considered, Stan can't call that safety.

The citizen, Douglas would have told him again (if

Stan hadn't mentioned his carrier bag), surrenders a certain amount of individual sovereignty, for the protection of life and property and the provision of essential services. But if government cannot provide these things, Stan sees, then their lives had held a fundamental lie.

He is, however, about to realise the protective nature of a house's walls. As a distant smashing sound begins and he hears the shouting of a voice, he looks about in the growing chill. Below the ornamentation, this is the truth: without a home you have nowhere to hide.

Hannah stands in the wind. From here she would be able to see everything, from Seven Sisters to central London under the orange night sky, but she's looking down, at the man who's throwing himself over and over at the front door far below. He has a hammer in his hand but he's ceased to use it.

'*Bitch!*' he screams repeatedly. The word is drawn out by the distance.

Up here, Hannah and her friend hear only parts of it.

'He's very angry...' she gradually remarks.

After exiting her afternoon with Stanley Donald Parsons, Hannah surfed the whisky back to her home – and now, as he sits staring like a fisheye through his empty bottle lens, she's leaning out from the building's ramparts into late night air, *Titanic*-style. Hannah lives with fifteen other people in the abandoned theatre that stands marooned on a traffic island at the base of Highgate Hill.

The small block from which its hulking shadow climbs comprises a minicab firm, a charity shop and a church, which at night burns a green neon crucifix. You must cross at least one of Archway's wheel of roads to get from any pavement to this building's door.

The theatre's windows are narrow, frosted-glass fingers, decorated with graffiti, punctuated by jagged holes. Its main entrance, which has slowly been bill-posted into obscurity, remains padlocked and unused. At the rear of the building however, through a chain-link alleyway, the back door can be found. Here there are no doorknobs, no keyholes at all, but only the blank steel of security, dappled by stickers that declare the immorality of Coca-Cola.

The only concession to the usual accoutrements associated with front doors comes disguised in the form of a piece of dirty string – hard to make out against the grey-sand brickwork, it dangles just within reach, four or five foot to the right of this blank armature. And it ascends four storeys, more than forty foot, snaking in through the small open angle of a window, where it's tied to a stolen last orders bell haphazardly screwed to the mortar of the wall inside.

The only way to get into the theatre is to be let in. There must always be someone at home; according to the then Section 6 of the only piece of British law Hannah was interested in; a property occupied is a home, and a home comes with rights, for anyone else claiming ownership must then pursue eviction through the courts, presenting deeds of proof if they wish to remove those who've made themselves resident. A property left without inhabitants however is no one's home and then sledge hammers can be used if the real owners see fit, to break any locks the squatters might have left in their stead while going out to buy a pint of milk, or get a job. All squatters are shackled to their makeshift homes. There's always somebody in at Hannah's place.

The vestibule entrance hasn't been used since 1989, but the man on the pavement rams his shoulder against the Coldplay posters without hesitation and the broad doors rattle in their frames.

'We can call the police.' Her friend's face has a yellow shine in the sodium night.

'You think the police are on our side?' Hannah responds.

'He can't get through there anyway though...' She licks her lips.

'Don't worry,' Hannah tells her.

The problem is not really happening now – it actually happened four weeks ago, when Hannah took the opportunity to walk out of the man's Finsbury Park flat while he was taking a shit. Specifically, it happened as she decided to carry with her the four hundred and sixty pounds and three small rocks of crack that he had in a box under his bed. He'd pissed her off – asking tirelessly, aggressively and with an assumed monopoly on ethics – when she was going to make her sexuality exclusively his. As she'd tried to explain to him a hundred times though, she believes in sharing.

He'd pissed her off, but not as much, it turns out, as she'd been able to piss him off in reciprocation. Really, the most surprising thing about this surprise visit is that it's been so long in coming.

The man's name is Mike. He's a white guy who grew up in Canning Town. He has heavy connections but Hannah's fairly sure that he's out on a limb with them right now. He's come alone.

When she has asked herself over the intervening four weeks – as she no longer has time to do – just exactly what her reasons had been for so unapologetically fucking over a man who'd declared his love for her, the only excuse she's been able to cite is freedom. The freedom that feels like this; this raised heartbeat, this adrenaline. Like the cool, clean air in front of the *Titanic's* prow.

'How long do you reckon before he gives up?' her friend asks.

'Depends on how long it's been since he ran out.' She has told Ciara the story. At the time of telling, Ciara had enjoyed a titilated laugh – and the crack.

'Someone else will call the police anyway,' she suggests to Hannah now.

Hannah's eyes skim the horizon for blue lights but only the green of that great, glowing crucifix adds colour to the view. Against the buildings' dark faces, it shines out with the tactless self-belief of a truly insignificant logo.

Mike's second name is Brown.

Mike grew up in a small house on a small street with small gardens, opposite a very large block of flats. At first, when he'd been small himself, those flats had been occupied, but slowly occupation had drained away. He's not sure – no one in the street had really been sure – whether the council had controlled the gradual evacuation of Park House or whether it had been voluntary. He remembers the great sign and its leisurely deterioration:

UNITS TO LET
181 377 1154

as if the words and numbers had held some code. When you're a child, everything has a secret meaning. Even as he's grown up, it's been hard to shake the notion that an indiscernible message had been hidden in the vast slogan that had ruled his view from ages nought to twelve. At the age of twelve, Mike had seen the sign removed and driven away on the back of a lorry – and for another decade, this had remained the only authoritarian intervention in Park House's destiny. Its destiny had been decomposition. The concrete walkways that had embraced its exterior had steadily grown a darker grey. Its board-covered doors had enclosed a world of mystery – and loss – like one of the time-capsules that Mike had made in his first year at high school and buried beside his classmates', in the little square of wasteland behind the school canteen. Through the formative years of his life, Mike had wondered about the left-behind mugs, the blank mantelpieces and slow-peeling wallpaper that must have been concealed inside Park House. And when he'd been old enough to take charge of his own life, he had made himself the master of its halls.

He'd been ten years old when they'd first broken in. With his friend Billy's crowbar, they'd easily popped the fixing from the front door of number 02. As they'd oohed and aahed and sworn for luck, the padlock had swayed little, decreasing arcs – and the liberated door had swung in, on blackness. Mike still remembers. Like it was just this morning, he can still feel the squelch of long-wet carpet underneath his Nikes. He can still smell that smell – of people long gone and the mess that people leave behind.

All the sinks in Park House had been full of dirty water. From flat to flat, down the straight, deserted corridors and in and out of every little room, the boys had travelled secret routes and made themselves a kingdom – where every sink had simultaneously been trickling onto every unused, neatly-fitted carpet.

This was the day that Mike had realised he could make the world his own. Before, life had seemed to be dominated by that commanding yet somehow suggestive sign:

UNITS TO LET
181 377 1154

which had governed the universe he knew. But on the 3rd of March in 1989, Mike and Billy and Psycho John and little Ed had come to know the truth. No matter how large the lettering, or how it seems to speak to you, a sign is not really a commandment from on high. It's a last request, in the wake of which, the commander has always departed.

In the years since, he has put this wisdom to good use, ignoring signs wherever he comes across them. Sometimes – as in the case of little Ed – this way of life can lead to prison. But Mike would rather risk a sentence than accept one voluntarily by doffing his cap to every lingering directive erected on the signposts of the world. He imagines that once a race of aliens ruled London and Essex. As they'd glided along their conveyor belts and back into their shining hatchways, they'd taken a last glance over the large red notices they'd left behind and nodded in satisfaction to themselves.

Perhaps unfortunately for Mike – and to a lesser extent for Hannah – in a world where rules must not be heeded, there is still a ruling class. Their weapons are not uniforms and prisons and courtrooms, but far more insidious tools: crack has come to rule Mike's life. And he thinks now that perhaps, in some way, his childlike mind had known better than his adult mind does. For he himself has become one of the many

UNITS TO LET

which are scattered throughout the occupied world.

He had thought that he might be in love with Hannah, but it's quite easy to fall in love with an idea. And Hannah is clever: she leaves little signs on her face and never qualifies them with anything that might be the truth. At least she thinks she's clever. But Hell hath no fury like a crack addict scorned. Mike knows now that he was not in love with her.

For her part, Hannah was always fully aware that she was not in love with Mike. As she often tells people, love is a four letter word. Hannah has spent much of her adult life avoiding love, alongside employment and sobriety. She has declared herself an untamed continent, trading with the richest visitors and laying mantraps just beyond the shore. Once, a very long time ago, she was invaded. Now, over even the slightest possibility of colonisation, she finds herself unilaterally choosing war.

Unfortunately for Hannah tonight, no one else is on her side. Of the twelve people who reside in the theatre with her and Ciara, one significantly attractive Brazilian man might have been relied upon, but right now he and all the others have gone to find them a new home. Their eviction date is only three days hence and it can be quite difficult to locate an empty building suitable to house fourteen.

In the meantime, Hannah and Ciara are holding the theatre. They both have mobile phones and up here the reception's pretty good. But who is she going to call? The boys will have all theirs turned off, not wanting to be interrupted at an inopportune moment, say when they're halfway through a window aperture. And she can't call the police. For one thing, every time she sees them, they take her into custody, and this has left her trust threadbare. For another, to do so would be to compromise the theatre's defences, for the police will most certainly want to come inside. And each of her housemates' possessions – many illegal – are still locked in below. The steels doors currently protecting her from Mike's hysteria are also the only things that would stand between the group's belongings and the capricious will of the boys in blue.

Mike has so far failed to look upwards, Hannah sees. Ignoring every sign he passes has left him with this habit.

On the pavement where Stanley sits, glancing nervously – despite the fact that the smashing noise is distant – there are other miscreants emerging. Two dark marionettes have come to sit on the bench a hundred yards away, White Lightning bottles aligned by their feet opaquely. A man in a long and dragging coat is walking the edges of the buildings, maybe searching for fag butts, like Hannah does – maybe for cash. He takes a detour into each phone box and scours the rejected-coin trays. And Stan has noticed that the 'special' phone box, which he sits in front of, is becoming operational now. Two girls in ten minutes and a visit for each: from a black man with a shabby face and short dreadlocks, whom Stanley might once have crossed the road to avoid.

Just as Hannah had warned him, the crawly people are beginning to come out of the walls. It is now approaching half past two in the morning – a time at which he and Claire would most certainly have been in bed – and the knot of patient service users that had gathered round each bus stop has now broken, each of them to find their slow way home. The kebab shops have closed, though their sapphire lights burn on in an emptier street. And Stan wasn't wise enough to ask them for leftovers. He's starting to feel less and less wise. The traffic has ceased to flow, the dark tarmac now nothing more than a consistently-decorated piece of ground.

Looking up – for Stanley's still enamoured with signs and hasn't yet learned that more is now to be gained by staring downwards – he sees that the windows which frame Junction Road's upper storeys are unanimously dark. Un-curtained. As though there are no inhabited apartments here, and all that exists above the now fallow shop-floors is an endless chain of units to let.

At night, Claire had always slept soundly, thanks to Nytol (though she had seemed to suffer a constant underlying cold). At several points, Stan had tried to raise the question of whether one could become addicted to such an innocent supplement, (often while Claire had sat in her nightie at the bedside, dispensing to herself), and such attempts had usually ended with the careful placement of a six inch gap between their reclining bodies. Stan himself had never touched the stuff, though he'd regularly suffered difficulty in sleeping. It was preferable to lie awake and bored than to enjoy the lulling dreamlessness of Nytol, as his wife did every evening. And who could tell now whether her reliance on such inoffensive remedies had contributed to the growth of those anarchic cells? Perhaps Claire's body had begun to rebel against its sweetly perfumed, strictly scheduled life. After all, he did not have cancer – as far as he still knew.

As it was, Claire had spent the hours of 22:30 to 05:45 in a world that Stan had never seen. And he had lain beside her, wondering aimlessly who else out there might also be awake. Sometimes counting sheep. Sometimes counting the hours until the combination of Natravene and the previous night's dinner had roused Claire once again into the life that they had shared.

Insomnia is a lonely sickness: a failure in yourself. What can be wrong with a person who's unable to rest when rest is such a natural requirement? Sometimes Stan would slip in and out of a dream-state without ever seeming to close his eyelids. And in this dream-state, normal things might seem frightening. Like the slow cycle of the boiler below them, or the gentle red radiance of the digital clock's numbers, reaching in through his open eyes.

One night he remembers sitting up and switching on his bedside lamp. Claire had slept on, the whole world meaningless to her, and he had reached over to take from her own bedside table the little bottle of Nytol, still in its box. He had surveyed it, as one might an enemy – though judging by his wife's opinions, it might well have become his friend. The list of its components had been long and unintelligible – and Stan had stroked Claire's thin and fluffy hair as he'd set it back in place. He wouldn't rely on a crutch like that – though he never would have named it such in front of the woman he loved.

Now he has no need to sleep. And he is learning how many other people have been awake at the same time as him. In fact, there has been a whole society out here, in the hours between dusk and dawn, with its own economy and system of law, to take the reins of command while Nytol works its shift over humanity.

'He's going to the other door...'

'He can't get in there either.'

He can't get in anywhere; they live in a fortress. Mike stalks its outskirts with his blood pumping bitterly. It's taken him four weeks to track Hannah down and during this time, a man called Ken has visited him on three separate occasions. Ken is in his forties with a bald head and a very expensive car. His brother, John, has just made DC in the Islington constabulary, which is one of the many reasons that Ken is gifted with such a broad smile. The friends he brings with him to Mike's flat in Seven Sisters do not smile. They like to step out of the Merc in synchrony. The last time, yesterday, Mike saw them coming and climbed out of the bathroom window to run between the alleyways of the Finsbury Park estate where he now lives. Returning five hours later he'd found the words *CALL ME* scratched with inch-deep gouges into his front door. Touching the lettering with the tip of one finger, Mike had pictured Ken's untroubled smile in the August sunshine – shaking his hairless head as the others had worked with diligence at the wood above Mike's letterbox.

Now he is beginning to reach the end of his tether and after a few moments' pushing at the steel door to the theatre's rear, he takes out his mobile phone. First he scrolls to the directory of 'H', which glows with a neon green not dissimilar to that of God's. Hannah is, for obvious reasons, the first name offered to him.

The phone – which has a seven centimeter full-colour screen, video capabilities and five hundred free minutes a month to other T3 mobiles – shows him a tiny little picture of a ringing handset as Hannah's pocket begins to vibrate.

'Fuck, it's him.'

'So don't answer it.'

'What difference does it make?' But for a few seconds she hesitates anyway. On her own T3 mobile a little picture of a spotted backside fills the high resolution screen. The polyphonic sample of a barking terrier begins.

'Fuck, fuck, alright.' She holds a flat hand to Ciara, who wasn't about to speak, and puts the phone up to her ear. 'Mike!' she says.

'Let me in.'

She cups her hands around the telephone's slim plastic. 'Let you in where...?'

'Open the fucking door, Hannah.'

'I'm in Madrid... ci, dame uno, valle, nada más... How are you, Mikey?'

'Alright, how about this like – I'm gonna hang up now. Then I'm gonna call Ken. I'll let him know where I am and we'll see him in five minutes, yeh?'

'Mike...'

But the phone goes dead in her hand.

Far below, in the chain-link shadows of the theatre's entranceway, Mike's hands are shaking slightly as he keys in the brightly illuminated letter K.

Ken is drinking a pint of HB in the Rose and Garter while his wife, Chris, watches a re-run of *Ten Years Younger* on its widescreen TV. Here, the cigarette smoke shifts in the air currents of any movement. Its nicotine soaks slowly into the fibres of the vast, white teddy bear that stares back at Ken from behind the bar, encouraging him to guess its name for the sake of Great Ormond Street's children.

In a neat line beside him sit John, Dave and John, each of them with an untouched half of Coca-Cola.

'Na, see,' John is saying to Dave, who's nodding, 'what you got to do is get yourself in trim mate, you don't want to be walking round with a gut like that; get yourself a George Foreman Lean Mean Grill Machine and have a look what pours out the side, you'll see –'

As the woman on *Ten Years Younger* lies back to have her anaesthetic administered, Ken hears the muted but recognisable notes of The Eagles' timeless classic *Take It Easy* – and putting down the beer slowly, pulls out his own T3 mobile.

Simultaneously, but unbeknownst to Stanley, Hannah, Ciara, Mike, Ken, John, Chris, Dave and John, a woman who wishes to remain unidentified is holding her own T3 to her ear.

'It's gone quiet, I don't know if he's left or what. I think you should send someone *right now*.'

Her curtained windows let the streetlight in like milk through muslin. And in their folds, her index finger holds one eyelet open: the road a shadowed, unfamiliar world.

The average response time for a police unit in Archway – which needs only to travel from the station on Holloway road – is an enviable two and a half minutes. However, the Rose and Garter is a similar distance away.

Ken and Ken's friends have already taken their places in the midst of the Merc's beige upholstery. Pulling out of the empty car park in Gospel Oak, its two and half litre engine carries them forward like a magic carpet. Ken's hands are calm between his large, still knees.

'We need to go,' Hannah says.

'What? Outside? No fucking way– '

'Now.'

She turns without glancing at Ciara's unbelieving face and pulls open the rooftop's door. 'The toilets...' Which possess the only windows in the building that can be used now – made of wire-meshed glass, that still open, being as they can be locked from inside.

They take the stairs two at a time, boots splattering the puddles collected in each hollow step. The theatre is like a giant Brita Filter, channelling London's rainwater through its ceilings and floors to gather, undisturbed, in each abandoned corner.

What was once its central auditorium – a great circular space, two storeys high and ringed by the balconies' red velvet seating – remains, but a spectre of its former self. Across the now-bare concrete floor, the two girls chase escape. Past the high stage, still intact but dark, and graffiti-covered walls. Between the rearing stacks of second hand books that Olly, their housemate, collects here and sorts – and sells from a shopping trolley by the nearest stations. The overriding scent is that of mould and the echoes still fall with a theatre's deep acoustics.

Hannah and Ciara run.

Not far away, Stanley raises his eyes in fear towards the police car's siren.

And Mike, who hears it too, ducks suddenly behind a pile of rubbish sacks, which luckily the squatters have not yet moved.

In the Merc, Ken and John and Dave and John emerge around the road's last corner, which might have been silent if not for their engine, and the screeching police tyres, and the sudden welter of voices and footsteps, and the violent thud of car doors.

This is a classic case of big fish, smaller fish.

Throughout London, the UK and beyond – perhaps in every instance of society – men like Ken have shaped events and led the species forward. It's not necessarily Ken's fault that, since the age of seven or eight, the world he's experienced has only seemed right when he's been in command. At that age, at least six inches taller than the other boys he knew, he had chanced upon the feeling of supremacy that would later come to dominate his aims; removing from his friends' possession their collections of cigarette card football heroes, he had made a startling realisation. By controlling the redistribution of the cards in a way that was more fitting, he was also able to control the hierarchy of his friends. This had made Ken feel good.

He was impressed by the way that order came immediately, to regulate the boys' relationships and reduce the rate of squabbling and scraps. He was encouraged by the greater fairness of a system of wealth which sprang, not from the random chance of being born to chain-smoking parents, but rather from the merit of the boys themselves. With their currency stored in a locked box underneath the bunk bed he'd shared with his brother, his friends had found far greater reason to show ambition. In seeking to prove themselves to Ken, they had regularly achieved heights of strength and loyalty previously unknown. And the most curious – most exciting – element of his discovery was the fact that none of them seemed to mind very much. After the first few days when the possibility of mutiny had grumbled around, each boy had begun to accept the situation. They'd all seemed quite happy with the idea of working to regain what they'd already owned. They had reapplied themselves with vigour to the task, as if the value had never lain in the cigarette cards at all.

Ken's chosen commodities no longer bear the faces of football heroes. In the import, manufacture and distribution of crack cocaine, methamphetamine and heroin, he has found the possibility of almost limitless control over those who freely choose to enter the competition. Ken does not indulge in the products himself – much as he was never interested in football. A heart-swelling, adrenaline-engorging rush of oneness with the world can be produced by something far less compromising: Ken has chosen power as his path and, perhaps surprisingly, everyone he's met along the way has supported his decision.

Of course, Ken knows his limitations. His brother, Detective Constable John Clint Saunders (who is, obviously, neither of the Johns now stepping out of the Mercedes) has always been two years older and has consequently acted as stabilising force on his ascent. Poring through the metal box – unlocked and spilling its cardboard secrets out across their bedroom floor – Ken had won John's seal of approval right from the start, on the grounds of law and order.

John, never having shown much interest in socialising, let alone in asserting his social position, was charmed to discover that by agreeing not to tell their parents he could install himself with one easy step above his brother.

Ken's friends were behaving with far more discipline than before, John was suitably assured. And for this reason John had allowed Ken to continue. The gift of this licence had made John feel good.

The issue of who's really in charge – John or Ken – might only be a question of perspective. Undoubtedly the Rose and Garter is some kind of powerhouse; gathering and issuing its influence onto the streets of North London. But it isn't difficult to see that HMP Pentonville, with its high, undecorated walls, holds an authority to outrank it.

Embedded in the prison's architecture, the shape of dominance can clearly be made out. Its windows form a gratifying symmetry, where they can be seen above the walls. It stretches equidistant arms from its imposing gatehouse. Solid, immovable – just like the ground itself.

However, it's often argued by Ken (for instance, when they get drunk at Christmas), that really it's the criminals who hold the upper hand. Justice is nothing more than the control of injustice, and it's the work of men like Ken that's lent injustice such a value as to make the control of it worthwhile.

Hannah and Ciara climb out of the window and proceed to run down Junction road. They are very small fish.

Mike camouflages himself with the detritus of the rubbish heap and remains in one corner, trying not to breathe. Though he's larger than either Ciara or Hannah, he is still smaller than John, Dave and John.

John, Dave and John stand, confused and unsure, as they see a band of policemen running towards them. They glance at Ken, who eases himself from the Mercedes and surveys the situation; by anyone's estimation a fairly large fish, or a shark, but not a whaler. He has no permit for these seas.

As the group convenes in the theatre's long shadow – the cops coming to a halt, as none of the men they see are fleeing – there's a long moment of assessment, a circular glance, during which each finds their level.

'Alright, Ken?' the first policeman says. 'We've had a call about some disturbance.'

'Everything's under control,' Ken answers.

'You involved in this, are you?'

'Involved in sorting it out.'

'Alright…' The policeman puts one hand to his walkie-talkie but doesn't use it, the gesture seeming to suffice.

'Going to have to ask you to disperse now, I'm afraid though.'

'Disperse…' Ken repeats the word. Seems to savour its image. Life-forms gradually floating away underwater. Gazing around, he doesn't see Mike, nor the girl who has Mike's money. So it is that, recognising each other, the powers-that-be remain in harmony, while those who are good enough at running or hiding retain their freedom and the natural order of the world prevails.

'What's wrong…?' Stan says, as Hannah dashes towards him, his own eyes nearly wild with the sounds of commotion and the knowledge that he himself is a wanted man.

Ciara stumbles to a halt behind, as Hannah says, 'Stanley Parsons! Nice to see you! Listen, I may need your help… I'm looking for somewhere to stay. We are looking. Right now. Where's this house of yours?'

Stanley's taken by surprise. And he's not a mean person. And besides, he has little to lose. So he describes to Hannah and Ciara the location of the building that he and his wife had once called home.

He watches them make for the Vorley Road turning and hot-footing it out of harm's way. And he suppresses the sense of sadness that rises, cold as seawater in their wake, with the thought that good intentions must bring good outcomes. Despite all that's happened, deep down Stanley still believes that good intentions make the world go round.

DAY # 3

It makes perfect sense. There are always bottom feeders.

Stanley opens his eyes. He remembers Claire's selection of herbal teas. Above him, the sky is blue. A day to make men whistle as they go to buy the papers. The blue of a California Stan's never seen. Of unsung possibility.

Just below the sky, but still above Stanley, is the rest of the world. The brickwork – reaching up to where the pigeons shift and stare. The doorways, reaching up into that brickwork. And in fact, the steps that run towards those doorways – Stan looks up at everything. A thought is born inside his mind.

He could be anyone today.

Of course, it's not true. His role is determined – by the events that have happened, and by the roles that everyone else fulfills. But as he rises into a sitting posture and the architecture of N19 slides into its upright position, he cannot shake the notion that all this is irrelevant – and that he could be anyone. Like anyone else could be.

He is very hungry this morning, very thirsty. He had thought that he'd been pretty hungry and thirsty yesterday but it turns out that that was nothing more than mild desire. Now he's really experiencing the burn.

People are passing already, often holding snacks. He thinks of the squeak of the kitchen's chequered floor tiles and can imagine, with utter precision, the way the fridge door feels as he opens it.

Coffee can be a good way to start the day; macchiato, filter, latte. Nutritionists advise breakfast, though their specifications differ, sometimes widely enough to form the basis for radio phone-in shows. The metabolic rate and consequently productivity is raised by the traditional morning meal, in the twenty-first century as ever.

Breakfast-on-the-go has become very popular, Stan considers as he sees the swift pedestrians, spawning muesli bars, and brunch pots, giving rise to the Egg McMuffin and porridge served in disposable cups. Claire had enjoyed drinking a different herbal tea each morning, favouring chamomile and honey on a Saturday. Perhaps it was because of the wide selection available at breakfast time that he'd never previously woken up feeling like his identity could also be a matter of choice. He'd always been a black coffee man. Now he doesn't have the option, he supposes he can be any kind of man at all.

Today he is a bottom feeder, but what does this mean? This unprecedented hop into a new role? What does it mean, if not that roles aren't solid?

The wind is light and warm. It carries air from unknown places and the people who inhabit London rise to reassume their lives, in just the places they left them yesterday. But they needn't, Stan thinks. All that's holding this city to its promises – that today is Saturday, that this is the United Kingdom, that he is Stanley Parsons, not Gregory or Jane or Douglas Johnson – is the people, who've agreed between them. His perception has shifted, uncontrollably.

It makes perfect sense: excess is bound to create bottom feeders and there's certainly excess here. It fills the stockrooms of the shops and every shelf, it circles in delivery vans around the city's streets and overflows its bins. Of course there are men like Stan to pick it over. This is reality, he thinks. He has never experienced it with such clarity. He pictures himself as a small bird, searching scraps from the edge of a pile so high it can't be fathomed. And he wonders at the distance between his feelings and that summit, which must be made of logical, evolutionary steps.

Stanley stands and looks across the road at his new kitchen. Just above it, wasps are flying in the air.

Beside the Co-op's green skips again, with only a cursory glance over his shoulder, Stan lifts each lid with expectation creating bubbles of hunger in his throat. If he takes the food out and walks away with it quickly enough, perhaps no one will see what's going on. And indeed, new, full bags lie amongst the torn plastic and cardboard of a supermarket's waste. Stan's fingers swim into the plastic, stretch and tear, and before him lies a selection of sandwiches. Some coronation chicken, some lamb with mint. Their packages intact, their use-by dates still a day hence, they're perfect, but unlike yesterday a type of bright blue fluid has been poured all over them.

Withdrawing his hands, they are stained. After a moment, taking this in, reaching for the second bag, he finds that its contents has also been rendered inedible: little pots of pasta salad with sweetcorn in them. The blue stuff looks like toilet cleaner. Staring at his fingers, Stan isn't sure.

He looks up at the busy pavement, realisation taking its hold. Each time someone passes him with a croissant or Mars bar, he feels like shouting. But his hunger doesn't change the fundamental rules of ownership. Short of begging, the need he feels can make little contact with the world around him and cannot change it in any way that might help him eat.

The people he sees are earning money – and now rightfully enjoying its fruits. He looks back down at his breakfast, which was never his, except in his mind, and begins to wonder again where he can get a glass of water. He thinks of Hannah and Ciara, waking up in his soot-stained ex-home.

His perception has shifted and it will not move back. All the taps have walls around them, with locked doors.

He approaches the kerb and stands amidst a loose band of people, watching for the pedestrian crossing's little green man. The traffic breathes in rhythm, waiting. The people walk. Everyone carries the gene for ambition in every stride.

They're changing the billboard up above. Sarah's minidisc experience has already disappeared. For the moment the frame is empty, but for the scraps of its previous lives. Stan feels wordless too as he crosses the road, taking advantage of one of the few systems which still serves him as well as it serves everybody else.

There must be something he can do.

He slept in just his shirt last night and wasn't cold, but now the August temperatures are taking their toll. Everyone has those new kinds of water bottles, with sports lids, sucking on them at any opportunity.

At about half past eleven, two Jehovah's Witnesses

come up to Stan themselves and hand him his own copy of the leaflet Hannah showed him the day before. Hesitating a moment, Stanley takes it and as he does so asks whether they know of a toilet he can use. They look quite surprised, which in turn surprises Stan. The Salvation Army will be open on Monday, they say.

'Why Jesus...?' he asks, once they've turned their backs and begun to walk away. '...Try whisky.'

A lot of people look round at him.

The Green Man will not give him water today, nor do they relent and offer him the use of their WC.

The sandwich bar/coffee shop that stands to Stanley's left, past Archway's underground exit, operates a 'no free gifts policy', he's told. But he knows this isn't true. Only a few weeks ago, he saw an attractive young woman pause outside the place with her dog. They gave her water, which she poured into a flattened carrier bag and indulgently watched the Labrador lap up.

Stanley has reached the point where his need outweighs his embarrassment and he doesn't care what the water's served in. He doesn't want a cup, he'll drink from the faucet or, if they don't want him to touch that, from a hole in a carrier bag. Apparently it's not the container that incurs the cost though. The value of water must be otherwise accrued.

It occurs to Stan that it's easier to help people who don't need help. Really needing help just doesn't look good and that seems to make the person giving it feel weird.

The billboard's replacement poster shows a smoothie.

The smoothie is made from red fruit. It is very large and the only thing in the picture. Perhaps six foot tall, it's hard to tell from this distance.

It is available from the Wild Bean Cafés which now adorn a select few of BP's many outposts. Stan is very, very thirsty. There has to be something he can do.

The lake in the peaceful new world – uncrumpled now that he has his own version – is not as blue as today's summer sky. Stan looks from one to the other and back again. It must be nearly thirty five degrees.

These are his options: he can beg, he can steal, he can ask random strangers whether they know the correct procedure or contact group for a homeless man who needs to drink and use the toilet, or he can go home. He must choose one of these four things.

He thinks it through. These are the words he could use:

'Excuse me but I'm homeless and I was wondering if you know who I should get in touch with?'

In his mind, it sounds quite reasonable but when he speaks it aloud, he has to admit himself that it sounds like a scam. Far more quickly and easily, he realises, he will get what he needs with the words: 'Spare some change please?'

He still resists. But with his gaze bobbing from face to passing face as though at sea, he asks himself why and has no answer.

At a quarter past twelve he realises that he cannot hang on any longer. He knows that it's quarter past twelve because, as he stands and begins to walk quickly towards the intersection, he sees a man on a mobile phone check his watch and speak this time aloud into the tiny receiver. Here and there around them, others look down at their wrists for comparison.

He hurries. He strides the crossings – Junction Road, Highgate Hill – and climbs the short wall into the park. No kids are playing.

He can hear two voices, not distant, but the grass is vacant; drying beneath the windows of the estate and surrounded by low bushes.

Stan ducks in and crouches, like he once did as a little boy amidst the sand dunes at St Davids. He pulls down his Marks & Spencers trousers and his Y-fronts, excreting without control. He experiences a terrible pain as it happens, both in his gut and in his heart, physical exertion, unhappiness and shame. The smell is rich without the Harpic freshened water. As he hears the voices grow a fraction louder, he feels like he might cry. He won't cry over this, because he's not doing wrong. He knows he hasn't yet sunk to the level which anyone who saw him might think he'd sunk to, for he is also disgusted.

He attempts to use the thick, evergreen leaves of the municipal shrubbery to wipe himself, pulls up and buttons his trousers and rushes away. Archway's centre visible again between the heavily laden trees, its shining roofs and hurried pavements, Stanley halts beside the sign. A simple pictogram of a terrier and its excretion, prohibited by a large cross.

Towards the end, Claire had become incontinent. As

the prerequisites of life had left her one by one, the ability to feed herself, to think coherently or speak, to control the working of her body, the equipment and drugs provided by the NHS had begun to function as a stand-in. It was technology like the catheter that separated us from the beasts. And Stan had wondered at the aims of palliative care, which looked as if they were guided by some unspoken etiquette. Because of course, although it was right to manage every aspect of Claire's journey towards death, it was not acceptable to exert any control over the death itself. At the very end, we weren't allowed to raise ourselves above the animals.

Why?

Stan steps down onto the pavement again. He doesn't know how he looks because he hasn't seen a mirror in four days but no one meets his gaze now. Amidst the well-oiled movement of the crowd, he seems to see Why? questions everywhere. Over and over, they float up like river weeds.

Above the streets, the Wild Bean Cafe smoothie is talismanic. Red.

Now his bowels are empty, his other needs have climbed on top.

The smoothie fills this distant view as if aligned by sacred geometry. With its crystalline beads of condensation, in its own fluoro lighting, it understands thirst. It articulates thirst – so well that no one else will ever have to. It is thirst personified.

Last night, Hannah and Ciara did not occupy Stan's house. This is because, though Stan walked out without locking and without taking his keys, protection has since been put in place for him. Before, the blue painted wood of the front door looked out from between cotoneaster and spirea. Now there's the grey and uninviting face of steel, matched by new steel window covers. It can be quite difficult to get a company like VPS to arrive on such short notice, unless you're calling from the Holloway Road constabulary.

The two girls stood there in the dark and exchanged no more than glances. Circling the building, Hannah searched for some chink in the armour, but with its installation being so recent, she found none. In the midst of the pleasant faux-Tudor exteriors that lined the rest of the street, Claire and Stanley's house was a blind box. The windows' new metal surfaces were perforated, allowing a narrow exchange of air from the rooms to the garden now that all the windowpanes had been broken for their bracings. Even standing outside, Hannah caught the scent of ash. Cupping her hand to her eyes and staring in through the perforations, she glimpsed a study pricked by a thousand tiny beams of yellow: across the wallpaper, across the desk, an old typewriter. In each corner of the room the cobwebs were magnified – embellished as though in a hammer horror movie with the clinging soot.

Returning to Ciara, who stood smoking a roll-up in the bushes beside the front gate, she said quietly, 'I know somewhere else. We can go but it's a walk. Maybe twenty minutes.'

Ciara concentrated on her cigarette. The Holly Lodge Estate, with its lawns and gabled entranceways, was as quiet as a goldfish bowl around them.

'I don't think I'm coming,' Hannah heard her say.

'No of course. Because you just smoke the rocks, not steal them.'

'This is not my problem, Hannah.' And to illustrate the concept of it not being her problem, Hannah watched her friend flick the dog end to the ground and stamp it out there.

'Go then.'

'I will.'

And she did. Down the silent unmarked road, between the other terraced houses, upon which, along with the streetlight, blessings of safety, warmth and comfort continued to rain unremarkably down.

Today it's sunlight that stipples the darkened interior of Stanley's house. The broken windowpanes litter every floor and glitter there like precious things. Unbeknownst to Stan, one of his four options is nonfunctional. Sickness was only recently in charge in this building but now, through the medium of DC John Saunders, the law has re-established itself; impounding all the taps and revoking Stanley's right to offer his new friend accommodation: 51 Oakfield Avenue is now the focus of a criminal investigation. Had Stanley gone through the official procedures, it might never have become such. Now that the investigation has been launched, it will be necessary for Stan to prove in court that he didn't administer too high a morphine dose or kindle the subsequent fire. Perhaps a lenient court might release him whatever the evidence shows, but for that to happen many facts must be ascertained and presented with supporting documentation. After all, no court in the land could acquit Stan on his say-so. There are a high number of necessary telephone calls, emails, requests and re-drafted statements. There is the matter of access to his home and the processes through which he must now go to be granted this, then the probability that Claire's charts and patient record have burnt away, and in the column entitled 'Aims', which had once held such hopefuls as 'build up patient's strength for next radiotherapy on 10th April', the final short entry of 'make patient as comfortable as possible' may no longer be available for any judge to read. There's the chance that Stan could get off, but only through the proper channels, and these are becoming increasingly difficult to pursue.

He remembers how organised Claire was. Had the situation been reversed, would she have stayed to deal with authorities? Perhaps she never would have believed it unfair. Maybe Claire had always understood that fairness is a very complicated thing.

For some days after he had seen it, Stan had remained silently troubled about the Strategy Solutions logo he'd seen, remotely issuing out on that nocturnal fax. When he'd finally found the right moment to ask Claire, it had been hard to shake the notion that it was a question she'd been expecting. She'd mimicked surprise and retreated to the inflexibility of her Nondisclosure Agreement.

Hours later, in bed, he couldn't stop himself retuning to the subject. Not only was Claire's expression uneasy, sufficient to make him worry about her, but in his own mind the image of the Ellipse Systems sleeping offices reverberated with a new, vague anxiety, at the frequency of the many electric bulbs that burned in blue throughout the Docklands night.

'Are we your clients then?' he'd asked her. 'Surely you can tell me that. What's the problem?'

'Why do you think they asked me to sign that agreement Stan, for fun? I could be prosecuted do you realise that?'

'For saying yes or no?'

'For compromising client confidentiality.'

'But you look worried...'

'Well that doesn't change anything.' She'd stared at her carefully French-manicured fingernails as they'd lain across the cover of *The Da Vinci Code*. Finally she'd spoken up. 'Do you know what Ellipse Systems manufacture?' she'd asked him.

Upon his subsequent silence, she'd finished, 'No I thought not', and had refused to speak about it anymore that night.

He did know what Ellipse Systems manufactured. Technology. In the end, what was the difference between one kind of system and another? They were all interconnected; they were all profiting from interconnectivity. Did it matter anymore what one small division produced?

Fairness in the UK is the product of many thousands of years of social evolution, but this is also something that could be said of gonorrhea. Gonorrhea begins with G.

As a result, Douglas Johnson knows quite a bit about it, and the galaxy and golf and genocide. He knows quite a lot about Great Britain (History Of), but rejects entirely the subject of fairness. Despite the fact that the contemplation of it occupied many of his hours as a child, it's such an intricate and convoluted idea that the inability to resolve it has eventually led Doug to abandon the notion altogether.

Sitting in the darkness of the hallway cupboard, nothing but the itching of his tights and the sound of his father's footsteps for company, it had sometimes seemed to Doug like fairness was a bright and burning goal – a concept of solidity. But the years since, plagued and finally conquered by the unwanted erections which had begun in his little Thinking Place, have left Doug far less sure.

It had seemed back then like fairness and freedom must be synonymous, and this is a belief that's persisted, like gonorrhea. But there is a beast inside Douglas, as there is inside us all, and the gradual realisation that the boys and girls he comes into contact with – and whom he's always wanted to help – need in fairness to be protected from him, has brought Doug to admit, with finality, that fairness and freedom are in fact quite separate things.

This morning Doug is sitting on the bench near Vorley Road again, beside a young tramp Stanley doesn't know. Perhaps twenty seven or twenty eight, his face is already ravaged and he has a bottle of White Lightning by his feet. Stan can't hear them from this distance but they're in a very animated discussion. Douglas is gesticulating with his arms.

As Stan approaches them, he hears snatches of their words between the traffic and can make out the anger in Douglas's movements.

'We had the right to bear arms in self-defence from the reign of Henry II until nineteen forty six!' Doug's shouting. He also knows quite a lot about gun control.

Stan's perhaps twenty yards away. He has realised that he's walking at a much reduced pace now, perhaps the first part of the long decline which ultimately leads to lying down.

'*Eleven eighty one until nineteen forty six!* But these rights no longer *exist*, since the UK's doctrine of parliamentary supremacy allows the repeal of previous laws with no exceptions such as are contained within a codified constitution!'

The young man, still sitting on the bench while Douglas stands and waves his arms, has slowly begun to shake his head in hopelessness, but it's hard to see whether it's Doug's state of mind or the reality of an unimpeded parliament that's depressing him.

'And it's best!' Doug declares with a flourish. 'It's best for everyone! Don't worry about that!'

The young man's gaze rises to Stanley's approach. Just as he's become less visible to everybody else, he's become more visible to the other people who have nowhere to go. Doug sees his audience's switch in attention and looks around himself. He seems irritated as he raises his hand and says,

'Davey, Stanley. Stanley, Davey.'

'Hello.'

'Alright,' Davey says.

'It's the never ending question...' Doug trails off.

In the thin shade of a tiny tree, Stanley sits – next to Davey's feet, and his White Lightning bottle. Douglas has suffered some kind of injury since Stan saw him last. There's a purple bruise discolouring his cheek. As far as Stanley can see, they don't have any food.

'We're discussing the right of the citizen to bear arms and the question of whether a government which disallows it is, by its very nature, oppressive,' Doug says. But even as he speaks, Stanley sees the man check him out for yoghurt too.

'People can't just walk around with guns, can they? What about Hungerford? Fuck.' Davey asks.

'Or Dunblane,' Stan adds.

And Douglas nods, his eyes refusing to assume the same trajectory, 'Exactly. But is the government sufficiently representative to justify its being armed against us? Is it a product of the people?'

Claire had continued working for Strategy Solutions unfailingly, despite the undercurrent of her doubts. With no foreknowledge of the swift, efficient changeover which would take place as soon as her illness manifested itself, she had often put in three hours from home in the morning, developing the access of one client or another. Sometimes, listening to her leaving messages on Manjit's answer machine at six forty five am, suggesting some follow-up call which she'd need to make or ordering some piece of research, it had been hard to imagine that Claire's health would ever fail. Stan had used to make her Ginseng and Raspberry tea on such occasions, before

96

trudging back to bed alone. Such had been the disparity in their routines. He'd found it difficult to recover even from one nightshift per week. Some days, they merely passed each other in the corridor.

Claire had not been a powerful woman, as such. Certainly, as they were to find, not irreplaceable in the workplace. But what she had lacked in influence, or salary, she had made up for in effort; completing each element of her job so well that she'd claimed satisfaction for her own.

Stan had carefully watched the influx of employees during each of his dayshifts at Ellipse. Remarkably few, considering the number of machines it comprised. He had kept an attentive eye on the CCTV monitor through which he had seen that fax appear – waiting for the moment when it would become obvious whose extension number it belonged to.

When they'd eaten dinner together, Claire's expression had been increasingly strained but Stan had drawn the line at booting up her PC himself when she was gone. No matter how his worries grew, he wouldn't overstep the boundary of her privacy – or undermine her in that way.

In the end though, it was she herself who broached the subject for the third and final time. Not long before the episode with the Sunny Delight – Stan supposes the cancer must already have been actuated – she'd come home from a day liaising and collapsed in a heap on the couch.

He had sat down next to her, with one hand on her knee.

'Can I make you a cup of Echinacea and Mint?' he'd said.

She had shaken her head – hardly heard him.

'Stan– ' she'd started.

'Yes?'

'I think I've done something... bad today.'

'Bad in what way, love?'

She'd shut her eyes and gently covered them with a hand, maybe just in exhaustion. 'I closed the Ellipse Systems contract. I can't do any more for them.'

'Well, from what I can judge, you've done them proud.'

'Oh yes,' she'd told him, 'yes there's no problem there. I'm sure I'll get a bonus in December. You know, I remember when I started this job – I wanted to help people. What a laugh,' she'd said. 'What a fucking laugh!' And she had never really sworn.

'How about wine?' he'd offered.

And she'd accepted. With the bottle beside them, they'd sat close on the sofa. October it had been, he thought. One way or another, the world had been dark outside, or as dark as London ever becomes. They'd had the gas fire burning – imitation logs – and the words had unwound rapidly in the comforting sound of its sootless, blue-flamed warmth.

Doug and Stan and Davey sit in slow triangular debate over the effectiveness of banning gun ownership. The sun is strong across Douglas's face and illuminates his madness clearly – the way he overdoes every expression, as though he's speaking to children, Stanley thinks – and also how he wipes his mouth each time he checks his carrier bag. The summer light is unkind to Mr Johnson.

'Can I have some of your cider, Davey?' Stan asks eventually – and he thanks God when the young man assents. Wiping his mouth, he continues to listen to Douglas's reheated tirade.

Fairness could be the most complicated thing that humans have ever invented, Stan thinks. Like the way the police constabularies are separated, in fairness to the people. They're talking about recombining them now, in an effort to make the exchange of information smoother. Certainly DC John Saunders might find it easier to gather all the documentation necessary to Stanley's trial if there weren't so many layers of bureaucracy to swim through. But even if he knew that, Stan might sit on the fence as far as this question is concerned. All systems must surely strive for fairness and therefore for obscurity of power. Who is he to say that all those layers of bureaucracy aren't the many interwoven strands of justice? It's not the fault of the courts that he can't get himself together. Interestingly, with every added strata of fairness, it becomes harder and harder to place the blame.

It wouldn't really have been fair to say that Claire had ever done evil. She had never perpetrated any truly evil act, like murder – the sort of thing that any fair place would have convicted her for. And yet, Stan knows, she went to her deathbed regretful about the final contribution of her working life, for in the end it had become impossible to deny that she'd played a part in the access development of evil.

When Claire had spoken the words 'remote viewing software' it had of course come to Stan that he *did* know what kind of technology Ellipse Systems manufactured – and that it was that. It had come to him, in a memory of Pete's voice, a little awe struck, slightly lecherous. Pete had loved his *Which* magazines.

Yes, he'd nodded slowly, as Claire had first mentioned the phrase. He *had* known. It was just that, much like access development, the syllables had never really added up to something he could get a grip on.

'…Of course,' she'd continued, her wine switching a little in the glass she had kept gesturing with, '… there are plenty of companies out there designing remote viewing software. Like any industry, it's a jungle. And it's access development that separates the men from the boys…'

Mike Brown's mother's home had been the last location in the entirety of Canning Town to enjoy a view of Canary Wharf and the Docklands. When, in 1992, the council had finally begun demolition and redevelopment on the carcass that was Park House, the Wharf's pale peaks and nightly illuminations had taken their place in the centre of his mother's living room windows – and bedroom windows, and bathroom windows in fact. It was one of the miracles of the Docklands renovation that, wherever you were in Canning Town, Canary Wharf would shine out somewhere in your view. Whether you sat at home or braved the multiple carriageways towards McDonald's or waited under the clear plastic and chrome of one of the many indistinguishable DLR stations, there it was: at the hub of every vista. It gave the high street a new dimension. There, where the curry houses and second hand mobile phone shops receded to a vanishing point, much as the giant cloud castle must have looked from the base of the beanstalk, Number One Cabot Square emerged, flanked by its ever-growing sisterhood.

Late in 2000, the ExCeL Centre had been completed and Mike had taken long walks round its outskirts. The exhibition space was constructed along lines not dissimilar to that of the Millennium Dome, but here the exoskeleton was far more solid: spider like. For a little while, his family had joked that finally Canning Town would have something other than the crime rate to earn it a place in the Guinness Book of World Records, but eventually these jokes had petered out. It became apparent that, although geographically the ExCeL Centre fell within the Canning Town locale, it was officially a part of Docklands. This became obvious when you strolled its perimeter, and yet seemed no less strange. Encountering two meter high gates and CCTV cameras, security guards and warning signs, you were assured that this was not a part of the Canning Town you knew. But, looking into the distance, three miles of waste ground and water separated Europe's largest exhibition centre from its high-rise motherland.

Canning Town had already seen many changes. It had never really been a safe or permanent home. Mike's mum had often shown visitors the spot, high up on the wall, where, beneath many layers of paint and paper, a waterline still demonstrated the apex of the flooded

Thames. It hadn't taken Mike or his family long to realise that, far from bringing an oasis of culture to their area, the ExCeL Centre was really the first sign of another encroaching tide.

New development can bring benefits – this is the trickle down effect. Had Mike seen fit to take advantage of it, the Jobcentre on the high street had amassed a window full of little cardboard adverts for construction workers. In this way, he might have been able to feel like a part of the redevelopment scheme. No one could say that he didn't have the opportunity.

It was hardly the fault of the Docklands' Development Committee that, by the time those ads had gone up, Mike had been far too interested in taking heroin in a derelict council block to have his ambition stirred by the prospect of employment on one of the many building sites of a future world.

Mike's mum often lamented the course that Canning Town had taken. When she'd been a girl growing up there, many members of her family had owned homes along the street and robbery, she said, had been impossible. To steal from one house, you'd have to make an escape through the gardens of every house that followed it – and the occupants had known each other then. No burglar would have made it further than three doors from his crime without being pulled up by a neighbour. Mike had nodded when his mum told these stories – a wistful expression on his own face. But in fact it had been a lucky thing that, during Mike's teenage years, no such community watch scheme had been operational.

Mike loves drugs – and heroin is the queen, though these days he only takes it for crack comedowns. In harmony with one another, they make the perfect partnership: smack, the beautiful blanket, and crack, the only world he wants to wake up into. He would never have entered his line of work if not for the beauty of narcotics. The love of them had been just about the only thing that he and Hannah had in common. When he occasionally goes back home to ask his mum and dad for money – and sees the look of disappointment in their eyes – he does wonder about other lives, other possibilities. Sitting in his old bedroom, which is their guest room now, he'll open the window to smoke a spliff and see the absence of Park House, remembering the golden days of his Empire. No one could really wish for the Canning Town of the past, but when Mike raises his eyes to the new, distant view, he can't comprehend how he could join the future.

The ExCeL Centre's website is very brightly coloured, cerise featuring particularly strongly. Soon it will host the *Star Wars* Celebration Europe – the first *Star Wars* fan event of its kind outside the United States. Claire had shown Stanley on her PC in the living room, taking time to demonstrate how the website's search engine featured no results for either 'Defence' or 'Arms' and pointing out its impressive pyramidal entranceway.

'It's a good website,' she'd said, incidentally. 'Ellipse's isn't bad too.'

'Uh huh,' he'd said, but to be honest he'd seen better ones with moving graphics.

'It cost four point four million pounds to police the DSEi event,' she'd told him. She had thrown her eyes to the ceiling when he'd asked her to remind him what that was, but he didn't live in Canning Town and he wasn't an arms dealer or a member of CAAT, so there was no real reason why he should know.

Remote viewing software is a highly valuable commodity. Its uses are many and varied and not all of them are to do with weaponry. For instance, it's a fantastic addition to mobile phones (Ken often enjoys a clip of a woman having sex with a prize bull on his T3 mobile). It facilitates networks of security cameras throughout the world (these, Ken also makes use of. He has three, of which he's very proud, positioned around the Rose and Garter's ramparts.) Just one of the many applications for remote viewing software is the guidance of long-range missiles – and perhaps it's not even the most lucrative. It is, however, not a sector of the market that could be ignored by any successful manufacturer, or any conscientious access development manager who happened to add a contribution to their business strategy.

Claire was conscientious – hard working since she'd been a girl.

Now, as always, the pedestrians drift past Stanley, Doug and Davey, travelling easily in black and white from the vision of one CCTV network to another: the Co-op's, the public transport companies', the police's, the Highways Department's, Tesco's, on and on. Thanks in part to Stanley's wife at least twenty percent of them are now facilitated by Ellipse's viewing software. This is quite low however, in comparison to the percentage of machines that bore the elliptical logo, somewhere small, often invisible externally, on the skillfully lit and column free 32,500 m^2 floors of ExCeL's Defence Systems and Equipment International Exhibition.

Mike was back in Canning Town for the week when the DSEi and accompanying protests went on. He gets back whenever he can; probably never would have left East London at all, but found in the end that it was easiest to go where the housing list took him. After four and a half years' waiting, Mike didn't kick up a fuss when he was finally deposited in Ken's manor instead of his own.

Mike's never owned a gun but a friend of his had a pistol once. It was heavier than he had ever imagined it might be. In general, Mike's not interested in armaments, on a personal or an international level. Though comedowns can make him violent, he's always been a passive man – he wouldn't have an opinion in the current discussion. Even if people were allowed as many guns as they liked, they wouldn't then be permitted to shoot burglars. That's fairness, give or take a TV. And of course, Ken would have a gun, whether or not they were licensed, or registered, or banned.

It was a mad few days, the exhibition, with police everywhere – and he'd been safe from all of them because he hadn't had dreadlocks or a sign. The strangest feeling ever, to walk round a place full of the old bill and feels as if you were in the free and clear. A mad few days – they'd shut a couple of schools down.

Freemasons Road had been a beehive. All over the Victoria Docks, people had swarmed. There'd been a lot of work available, security and catering, that kind of thing, but Mike hadn't needed the cash that badly. He'd still been on Ken's good side then. He'd sat in a café with a cup of tea for three hours one afternoon, just watching the people and police go by.

He couldn't get close enough to see what was going on at the Centre itself. There in the great concourses and echoing halls, much as in the Rose and Garter, the exchange of armaments went on unhindered by the turmoil of the outside world.

Sometimes Douglas reaches forward and shakes the collar of Davey's coat as he speaks in a way that makes Stan feel uneasy. Davey does nothing to resist it, only gazes at Douglas with a listless stare. He's too young to be here, Stanley thinks.

'In a civilisation where only the rulers have legal access to weaponry, the citizens can never be more than sheep – herded and penned and utilised and bred – but the majority must *want* it.'

Davey shrugs, 'Well what else is there? If everyone was allowed to run around with guns then the biggest bastards would run everything, wouldn't they, like they did in fucking medieval times.'

Stanley listens with a lost heart. Once upon a time, he supposes, Genghis Khan must have woken up feeling like he could be anyone today.

'And fairness – or democracy, as it's called when implemented by a higher power – isn't something anyone can be allowed to opt out of.' As, step by step, Douglas demonstrates each logical argument, his expressions grow wilder with useless rage.

You can see fairness everywhere you look: in the equally apportioned pavement licenses for areas outside each shop or the interchanging rights-of-way around the junctions, in the expressions of righteousness on the faces of the passers-by, each of whom may register their right to vote. And to some extent, Stan sees, you can make out freedom. It must be that his country has evolved in the correct way, in the natural way, and its laws – on toiletries or euthanasia – are of the best possible sort.

'We've created this system ourselves,' Doug is raving, 'through our many rulers and revolutions – the best system always wins! The grumbles of the people become... eventually, the tectonic shifts of their government. Slowly humanity has created this!'

And who wouldn't want to live in Britain on such an August afternoon? Portable charcoal grills are Buy-One-Get-One-Free in the Co-op this week. The god of results stands incarnate.

Stan listens to Mr Johnson, who is climaxing.

'...we *need* to be unarmed, and we *need* the authorities to be armed against us... we need the state to protect us from *ourselves!*'

He feels the sense of hopelessness that he saw on Davey's face as he approached them. There's no escaping the reason of the world.

Composed of everyone, perhaps the unavoidable sum of evolution, society was a giant 'Power Ranger' of results. He'd sometimes flicked past *Power Rangers* on the TV after his nightshifts ended and, although it was quite frightening – vast, mechanical, bright pink like the ExCeL Centre website – its actions were governed by justice and were to the benefit of all.

It's easy to see the excellence of Britain from the way that everybody else flocks to live here, Stan has thought. Two weeks ago, the television on as always, highly strung and constant, blanketing their living room with remnants of familiarity, Stan had sat with Claire's hand in his own and seen the nightly news. There had been riots in the detention centres of the UK.

Scattered across the country, encased in their own blank perimeters, not unlike those of Pentonville or ExCeL, these sentinels of prevailing British fairness stood to outlast any media storm. They were strange, Stan thought, in that they were there to uphold Britain, but what they contained was a kind of citizenless limbo-land. He had noticed the cameras – elegant and menacing and dark – and had wondered on which software they were running; but it was the tried and tested use of walls that really enabled the places to work. The outer ring of buildings encased a central yard, Stan had seen from a helicopter's viewpoint. The detainees had been corralled inside, in an effort to quell the riot, some time ago it seemed, for with their sheets they'd spelled out the word:

HELP

on the asphalt ground. Presumably their applications had not been failed on a lack of knowledge of the English language. They had to take such tests these days, he knew. But it wouldn't have been fair to British people, people like Claire and himself, to let just anyone catch a lift in a lorry from Spain and put their name down on the housing list. British people, like them, had paid their taxes, worked every day of their bloody lives to enjoy the benefits of Britain. These thoughts had turned through Stan's mind as the lettering across his TV screen had mouthed:

HELP

over and over at him. In his own hand, resting on the arm of the chair, Claire's palm had been light and cool, like his grandmother's when he'd been small. Most of the time she hadn't known whether he was touching her or not though. She slipped in and out of consciousness and if he was honest, it was a relief when she was unaware like this. The news item on the detainee camps had gone on and on. Perhaps the reason that the NHS was so much worse these days was the number of foreign people it had to serve. For a moment, Stan had imagined walls around the outside of the entire country, bare and white and manned by Ellipse. He didn't want that kind of world, but Claire was dying beside him and perhaps if she hadn't been forced to share, she wouldn't be.

How could he know? The 'truth' was too big to be one answer. There were so many different newspapers and they all said different things. All reports were commissioned by someone. How could anyone know what was right or wrong when fairness was so massive?

On the asphalt yard, the black and Asian people sat in ones and twos, surrounded by their own excrement. Beside him Claire had been lying, fed and watered, dressed in a nappy for her faeces, de-cathetered and still. He had shaken his head at the horrific images on the screen, both in disgust and pity, unable to imagine defecating in a public space.

Darkness falls. Not a hindrance to any security camera.

Saturday night is in full swing in London. Around their three still figures, everybody else is getting drunk.

Far away, on other continents, cluster bombs are lying in the night, nestled between foreign grasses and leaves. Missiles are impacting, with effects that Stanley was, until recently, almost incapable of imagining. In some ways though, he thinks, the pubs and the money that people have as they walk in are both essential services, and it's national security that protects the British people's right to them. How would he know whether wars are necessary or not? Or weaponry?

The revellers spill from the bars and onto night buses, which Douglas doesn't bother to try and hail. They flow with a coalescing trail of brake lights along the routes of the city's A-Z, to Old Street and beyond, engorging leisure districts and carrying each and every partygoer onwards, after, safely to their home.

He can understand that they don't think of wars or bombs that often – for instance as much as those in the detention centres must. Who would want to think of such things when it wasn't necessary to do so? What Stanley doesn't understand anymore as he watches them walking – arm in arm sometimes, in friendship or in love – is the way that they, and he, and Claire, could forget about their own approaching deaths so completely as never to realise that there was any alternative to life.

The shop windows sparkle with tantalising, lit displays throughout the night – un-purchasable. Stanley's gaze moves from one to the next. At regular intervals, as if the common factor to unite the cornucopia of every store, giant banners display the word:

SALE

DAY # 3 (Night)

Night hours are passing.

Stanley and Davey and Douglas Johnson are still outside the abandoned Abbey National. Two hundred yards away the great green crucifix shines out again, spread eagled: a quarter to three.

Stan makes his bed below the cash machine, with two blankets that Davey showed him how to retrieve from the depths of the Oxfam donations bin. While Doug enjoys unconsciousness, Davey sits on the bench beside him and whistles hits of the eighties to himself.

It is a clear and beautiful night with the radiance of passing satellites tracking designs for a new zodiac, far up above the wealth of London's lights. Stanley arranges the blankets carefully on the pavement.

The sight of his small bed brings a curious sensation. Though alone without Claire, he looks down at the blankets and the feeling embraces him. He'd never realised this street corner could be his bed. It's the strangest thing: a sense of oneness with the world.

Claire is lying at Menzies and Sons' undertakers in Gospel Oak in a temperature-controlled steel drawer. The earliest hours of Sunday morning are elapsing with the three slim hands of the clock that hangs above their dim reception desk.

Stan sleeps. He dreams of red smoothies. In his dream,

though, smoothies are intoxicating. As he puts his lips to the straw, which is also red, he thinks to himself, *why not get drunk?*

Mike is out at work.

Hannah and the Brazilian man she's squatted with for the past six months (who is very unlike Mike, and called Bernado) are breaking and entering.

Partly through a noble urge to keep the danger that has finally pinpointed her away from her friends, and partly through a slightly less noble urge to separate herself from the conspicuous pack with which she's already been pinpointed, Hannah has decided to leave the theatre's fifteen. Rather than attempting to explain to them who Ken is and that he might visit as soon as Mike tracks them down again, she has stolen Bernado, who was easily got, and taken him to assist her in opening this, a much more discreet, lower-key affair.

They have pried away the perforated steel plate that covers one of the windows of a two-bed flat on the Woodberry Down estate. Now they are about to climb inside. The window belongs to a bathroom and its loose-cornered panel had been the only flaw in an otherwise well-secured piece of council property. It's on the first floor but accessible – sort of – via a balcony. Bernado has a theory: there is always one flaw. 'VPS aren't stupid,' he says with a wink, 'they leave an opening, in case they lock themselves out.'

Eventually they will have to find others; a rota of two is insufficient for occupation, but it's enough to facilitate this easy little break, devoid of superfluous voices and silhouettes.

It looks like this:

The estate is an echoing long-shaded place where the buildings rear up close to each other, hung with darkened balconies and walkways. A three-lane Red Route Clearway divides Woodberry Down, both north and southbound routes, six carriageways in total, so that this part of the estate where Hannah and Bernado stand is walled in alone. Traffic and wind-struck tarmac partition it away from the buildings on the other side.

They are flat against the brickwork: Bernado on the balcony, Hannah standing on its handrail and reaching out, into the nearby window aperture. He holds her other hand, his face like an interesting ethnic mask with the effort of his silence. She is picking spikes of glass from the frame.

There are many empty flats on the Woodberry Down estate, it is one of the many estates in London currently undergoing the process of decampment. Though the buildings were only completed in 1962, structural problems and water-penetration have begun to end their lives. It can take up to a decade to decamp however, and here it has only just begun. At least eighty percent of its one and two bed apartments still have front doors instead of these steel plates.

Fifty years is not an unacceptable lifespan for such an estate though, as those overseeing the regeneration know. They were children when Woodberry Down was newly built and that was a long time ago.

Ken is at home watching *Cum Swapping Sluts 4* while his wife enjoys a night out on the town. His brother John, who does not agree with pornography, or find it sexually stimulating, is lying between the matching covers that grace his Hypnos bed while the Teasmade, quiet and grey on the bedside table, counts down the hours until its work begins; a twentieth century remodeling of Menzies and Sons' more traditional, roman-numeral-trimmed timepiece.

John Saunders doesn't have a wife but he does have a disposable income large enough to enjoy some of the same benefits. He was once engaged to a girl, but police work being what it is, their betrothal didn't last. He is a man of organised nature, who is prepared to dedicate a great deal of time to his career. Not only does his occupation benefit his own life but many other people's. For this, he has been willing to sacrifice a few of the comforts normal citizens enjoy.

John, like his brother, is a man blessed with a tremendous sense of his own correct placement in the world. He has never suffered nightmares. He doesn't fear the future. He rarely experiences jealousy. This is because he's doing what he was always meant to do. John doesn't believe in God but he does think in some way that an overriding purpose exists in the universe. Never having wanted to explore or deconstruct these feelings, John's spirituality lies vaguely beneath his vision of the world, sometimes seeming to take the form of a vast and beautiful net – or perhaps a database – within which every cell is exact and specified, fulfilling its own purpose.

He and his brother never talk about God – it's one of the many subjects that's out-of-bounds between them, pornography being another. Ken's very successful nightclub and security company being a third. John's continuing, seemingly inextinguishable desire for his brother's wife just one more in the long line.

John cannot talk about his longing for Chris, for reasons that dig deeper than Ken's feelings. He himself can't quite address the nature of the attraction. Chris is in her early forties now of course, as are both John and Ken. The desire has become easier to handle with their middle years. But many were the occasions, New Year's Eve parties, Boxing Days long ago, when John would watch Christine getting drunk and experience feelings that would lead him to go out for a quick, cold walk. Christine is not and never has been a woman of taste or elegance. Her blonde hair, her heavy make up and her clothes are of the kind that remind John far too clearly of the streets where they grew up. He doesn't want to kiss Christine or whisk her off to better places. He doesn't ever allow his mind to wander towards the subject of what she and his brother might do in bed. His feelings for Chris are perhaps the only elements in that beautiful net that haven't fallen in their correct and individualised homes as far as John's concerned. He's not one of the animals his brother employs.

Stan's case is only one of the many currently occupying John's timetable. For his part, John believes that Stanley Parsons is guilty of ending his wife's life prematurely. He passes no judgement on whether such an act is right or wrong but learned to trust his gut feelings long ago in the matter of suspects' guilt or innocence, and here he can see it unmistakably in Stanley's trail. John Saunders pursues the truth in the cases that are put his way. He has no interest in creating or abolishing laws. It would have been easy to visualize his own perfect place in the world as that of enforcer – the separation of enforcer and lawmaker constituting only another rightful strand in that huge and intricate web of fairness – but in fact, there are a lot of laws and not all of them can be enforced at once. All policemen are required to prioritise and in this way the rules become more flexible. It's a blurring of the lines that might have led to doubt or the weakening of John's vision of the world, if not for the fact that in moments of uncertainty he has learnt to trust to faith. For the strength of mind necessary to his job, he must act with the belief that his motions are somehow guided; just a part of the structure that holds the world in place.

Douglas Johnson sleeps with his carrier bag held against his stomach, underneath a filthy coat. The bag is heavy and its angular shapes make themselves known through his clothes. Tucked between the buttons, his sleeping fingers guard.

Davey spares a glance towards it, halfway through the second chorus of *A Harvest For The World*. He has known Doug for four months, give or take, and has never been offered a glance inside.

'...*when will there be... will there be... when will there be... will there be... (a harvest for the world?) when will there be... will there be...*'

Douglas grunts in his sleep, seeming at peace, but on the bag his hand is shifting. It does not contain food or alcohol, of this Davey is sure, or he and the bag would have been long-gone by now. Nor does it contain drugs, for Douglas doesn't take them. Its edges are far too hard to be spare clothing.

'... *half of us are satisfied... half of us in need...*' Doug's facial hair catches the streetlight in tiny glistening jewels. He reminds Davey a little of his grandfather. '*But when the la la la la-la... la la la la la...*' In the quiet of the empty road, Davey's voice slowly relinquishes the tune and starts on an Annie Lennox song instead.

Davey – or David Barnes, as he was born – is twenty four years old. It's three months since he's washed his body or changed his clothes, though he knows where these services are available each week. He finds it hard to keep track of Mondays when the Salvation Army opens its doors, but this isn't the main reason for his lack of grooming. What Davey's really missing is willpower. Two or three years ago things got out of his control. Willpower didn't help him and its failure made him so sad that eventually he withdrew from it.

David Barnes drowned. Now Davey lives here underwater, where the sounds of the world are muffled and the ever-shifting cycles of night and day don't require anything from him. He's scared to change his clothes, to raise the bar like that – clean clothes ask for maintenance. He doesn't want to make any promises anymore.

He watches people walk by in the street during the daytimes and has the sensation that he himself is missing something fundamental, something ordinary to everybody else. He doesn't know why he couldn't cope. Lots of people lose their jobs – they just get new ones.

One of his errors was pride, he thinks when he looks back. He set his sights too high in the first place. He could be team leader at a supermarket now – there are always jobs available in supermarkets – and he might still be renting, the bills arriving in manageable chunks. He never needed to dream of success. But his parents had had high hopes for him, it was only natural that he should pick up on that. Surely ambition is environmental too. Davey has ten GCSEs, three A levels and a degree in business studies but those things were achieved in a frame of mind he doesn't have anymore. He read that genetics story in the paper – he reads everything he finds, though he's usually too drunk to take the information in. Who in the world blames genetics for their own lives though, except people who are looking for an excuse?

His second big error had been panicking. Failure to adjust quickly enough – to adapt to new circumstances and survive. What they don't tell you when you lose your job – with a redundancy payment of six hundred pounds, which seems quite generous when you've only been there nine months – is that a countdown begins as you walk out of the office doors. It may feel as though you suddenly have a lot of time on your hands, but in fact this isn't the case in any way.

As David had said goodbye to the rest of the domainnames.com sales team and taken the tube back to his shared house in Clapham, his view of himself had remained undiluted – it was the world that had looked less solid. Six hundred pounds had guaranteed more than a month's security in his home, for his credit cards and bills, his mobile phone. It was a shock to see a position with such good prospects dematerialise, but he'd had every confidence in his ability to get another job. *The Guardian* had had so many listed.

He was surprised by failure. He'd always been prepared for success. Six weeks had elapsed by the time Davey was forced to readjust his sights and by this point he no longer had time to find employment with Asda. Delivering his application forms, not long before his rent was due, Jennifer, the team leader, assured him that they would be processed in two weeks. It was four before he heard from her regarding an interview though, by which point he was sleeping on the sofa at a friend's.

Paul's place in Stockwell was tiny and uncomfortable but he put up with Davey for a good five weeks. He still has some of his stuff in boxes in the garage now – clothes and the kind of things you can't sell. By the time Davey's interview at Asda had arrived, he'd been in a pretty dark mood. Really, he hadn't given it his all.

Around that time the credit card companies had started to enquire about cancelled direct debits. He'd left the unpaid electricity, water, TV, council tax and broadband bills with his housemates who'd responded, unsurprisingly, by refusing to answer the door to him. Unable to get his post frequently, it was easy not to be frightened until it was much too late.

Davey remembers sitting at Paul's cramped kitchen table – with access to a landline at last, his T3 contract cancelled. He remembers speaking to a debt collection agency and feeling glad that the Clapham address was behind him. He remembers calling the bank and asking for an overdraft extension – thinking the worst they could do was say no. The young man on the other end of the phone, who was still gainfully employed, had asked about Davey's vocation. After wading his way through an answer, he was informed that a two month period with no credit to his account not only prohibited an overdraft extension but also necessitated the recall of the current debt. With Paul out, the flat hadn't seemed any bigger. The windows were always misty; views of other buildings obscured.

'I didn't know you could do that,' Davey had said.

What had ensued then was a kind of siege situation, in which reality had won. He'd screamed at unmanned telephone menu systems each morning and hunted for short term jobs each afternoon. His desire to achieve had really been his undoing. Fighting each level of failure only left him searching lower down. It had been a decision on his part – of course it had – to stop trying. But it was amazing how things could slip away without you noticing. Nothing concrete even seemed to change.

The final step in David's transition occurred on the fourth night after he left Paul's home. Sleeping rough in Oval, in the middle of the night he'd awoken with two men pissing onto him. Silhouetted against the streetlamps, they'd kicked him in the head fifteen times before running away and Davey had lain undiscovered until the morning, when the paramedics finally came. He's a different person now. He's not interested in sales. He knows how he looks to the people who might give him work. Where before he had thought himself better than supermarket assistants, now, at eight o'clock each night, he watches them remove the logos from the out of date food as the fluorescent bulbs shine down on customerless aisles. He watches them fill the skips, and pour the Domestos in, and roll these hulking shapes into the alleyways. A lot of supermarkets use cameras to safeguard their waste, as Stanley could tell him though, none of those cameras run Pyramid software anymore. It's a rapid and changeable world.

Before Stan slept, sitting up between the blankets that Davey had shown him how to steal, looking at the profile of the young man's vaguely misshapen face in the shadow, he'd asked what it was that prevented Davey returning to his parents' home.

Claire had been unable to have children. Producing cysts instead of healthy eggs, her ovaries had made the decision for them. It was something that had never seemed to upset her – only in their later years had the quiet weekends begun to weigh heavy. She had said she'd always known she didn't want kids. And he himself – well, what was the point in desiring something impossible? Adoption or foster care had never crossed the threshold of their conversations. Somewhere deep between the many quiet layers of their marriage, he had sensed a fear in Claire: to want motherhood would have been to validate her inability.

Had their lives – or Claire's physiology – been different though, Stanley was certain that there would have been no line past which any kid of theirs would have become unwelcome.

Davey just sat on the bench without replying, the cider bottle held between his knees.

'Do you still talk to them?' Stan had asked him.

He had shrugged, his eyes on the windows opposite.

'They must miss you,' he'd said. But he'd begun to feel uncomfortable even before he'd finished speaking – trespassing. He'd looked away, perhaps only following the line of enquiry for selfish reasons. Had he and Claire started a family, the last six months might have been very different. Maybe now someone would be looking for him. 'You should go back to them,' he'd finished.

Davey had turned and gestured to where Stan was sitting, perhaps to the blanket that covered him, perhaps to his clothes or his face, he wasn't sure.

'Are you trying to tell me you haven't got anyone? Any friends?'

The names and faces of various couples had passed through Stanley's mind – people he cared about in fact. He couldn't blame his friends for not taking the place of their missing children at Claire's bedside.

'Yes. I've got friends,' he'd said.

Davey had nodded. 'But you haven't gone to their front door.'

Now, still, the three are reclining.

Silence and silence and Douglas' snores. Units to let in the emptying street.

Unbeknownst to Stanley, several of the people whose names occurred to him with Davey's question have already been contacted by the police. Having copied the addresses from the backs of the most text-heavy get-well-soon cards on the Parsons' mantelpiece and the torn envelopes in the recycling bags that had stood outside their door, DC John Saunders had found himself in the homes of those friends that Stanley hasn't gone to. Johnny and Jan Carter (whom Stan has known since Jan was the receptionist at Smith Corona, back in 1980 or '81) sat yesterday with Detective Saunders in one of their armchairs, listening to his short story open-mouthed. Death and fire and disappearance.

'...I tried to call yesterday...' Jan had said.

But how could Stan have talked to them that first night? His eyes had been full of the memory of Claire's body disintegrating. His head had been full of the sounds of *Family Fortunes*, oscillating and warping. He couldn't have gone to them. His fingers had been stained green-black by the liquid that had issued from Claire.

'There is nothing in living nature,' he'd thought this evening before sleeping, 'that is not in relation to the whole.'

The window dressings of the city would twinkle on throughout the night, eventually handing the streets back to the day. An entire world with the barest reference to death.

DC Saunders had looked into the dual holes of Jan and Johnny Carter's expressions.

'As you can see, it's for Stanley's own sake that we're trying to find him,' he'd said.

Hannah finds her purchase on the edge of the bathroom window's little shelf. She and Bernado are counting in synchronicity: one, two... three.

The flat is dark and damp and silent and every noise she makes is an intrusion here. The scratch of the loose glass on the shelf. The knock of her shoulder against the steel brace, her foot's first movement on the floor.

Property seems to gain its own sentience in the wake of occupation. From the rooms before her, Hannah feels the personless place breathe. She hears Bernado make his effort behind.

The bathroom's walls are regulated, narrow. Woodberry Down was purpose-built for fairness so every bathroom in every block here is the same. Each with their own orientation and their differing views of the little paved areas outside their windows, the kitchens and living rooms and balconies match measurements, as did the rooms of Park House where Mike spent all the days that are now gone.

Advancing into the tight hallway, she turns to see Bernado's shoulders and torso pushing their way through the hole. Everything outside looks bright by comparison. Hannah pushes the button on her tiny key ring torch: blue LED illumination. Three rectangular open doorways face the hall, plus the shineless steel of the Sitex in the front door's hole. Here, against the wall, the original leans.

'It's here...?' he's saying as he comes to stand behind her.

She holds the faint light onto its painted panels. He's so close she feels him nod as he puts the tool bag down beside her ankles.

They'll work into the early hours of summer dawn, as quietly as they can: removing first all the Sitex's hinges and leaving it, held in the frame by its own lock. They'll bar the window they came in through. Every other metal panel left in place, as the August light begins to cut the sky at four thirty, they'll see only the vague greying of the tiny dots that perforate each piece of steel. They will not test the lights.

It takes an hour for the two man security patrol team to complete their circuit of the estate. In their very own van with their very own logo and their very own twelve stone German Shepherd, equipped with matching company Mag-lites, they are on the look out for just this kind of thing.

Mike was also breaking and entering tonight but the home of his choice was inhabited. Like Hannah, Mike rarely concerns himself with the rules of ownership, which is one of the reasons John Saunders sleeps so sound in his own position. Citing Robin Hood or the general unfairness of the world – for fairness can so often seem unfair – Mike contents his conscience with a history of Great Britain somewhat lacking the detail of Douglas Johnson's version, and one he has never put into words.

Once upon a time, the strongest and most evil people took all the land and made the rest of the population into serfs. Unable to hold their baronies in total slavery for long, and busy making wars with each other too, they were gradually forced to conform to a whole, which was gradually forced to concede to a parliament and universal suffrage and a welfare state. But because the land, and therefore all the money, is still in the hands of their descendents, and because the system of democracy that has evolved from them is only a matter of concession, the concept of a just society based on earnings and ownership is bullshit and it isn't wrong to steal from people who are wealthier than him.

Douglas Johnson would have loved to tell Mike, as he'd once told many fifth-formers, all about this very subject – and in many respects he might have agreed. 'The industrial workers of the factories and docks were instrumental in empowering those who pressed for reform acts,' he might have told Mike, 'finally opening the vote to property-owning men and initiating DEMOCRACY in Great Britain. But of course the reforms didn't *give* them property, *no*, they would be forced into a new struggle: the quest for ownership.'

On the bench beside the station, Doug's head slips a little and lolls without control against his neck. Davey watches the bag move under the coat.

'It would be *generations* until these families could dream of real representation or wealth, but nonetheless, the machinery of the masses had brought about a change…'

Doug's eyelids flicker with the brush of dreams.

'So… Betty, what can you tell me about the corn laws?'

Though it's garnered many other forms of significance since the era when stone huts or mud and straw were favoured, when reduced to its primary elements a home is still little more than a protective container to which the rightful tenant has the key. And its basic purposes,

127

when stripped of aesthetics, remain unchanged: the rightful tenant can lock others out, they can lock themselves in, or they can leave it unsupervised, safe in the knowledge that they alone can open it again.

Bernado and Hannah have broken the two bedroom Woodberry Down flat. A broken building, however, is a container forced open, for which the squatter has no key. Sitex plates like the one currently fitted into the front door's orifice are made from steel and their locks can't be sawn out and substituted.

The original front door though – wood panelled, leant in the dark against the corridor wall – can easily have its Yale system unscrewed and removed. An appropriate hole is then revealed for the combination lock and deadbolt that Bernado brought, weighing like a fist through the pocket of his canvas toolbag. Forming a substantial part of his worth tonight, the Brazilian owns a fine collection of tools.

He and Hannah fit the new lockplate into the unattached door and, though it doesn't look wholly legitimate – chewed wood bare around the edges of its brass plate – it will nonetheless serve its purpose now. They move the door carefully into position. It takes just two minutes of cold air, distant traffic and dawn – vulnerability – and the two are exchanged.

And then they're alone in the darkness again, but now in tenure.

Bernado takes out an attractive Indian throw and they sit on the floor, in an area swept clean of broken glass by one of his sandal-clad feet. Possession was nine tenths of the law.

The names of the security guards tonight are Frank and Leroy. Men of pride. They have been briefed.

Woodberry Down must be patrolled, or every one of these shuttered homes would become illegally occupied. The process of decampment and regeneration would be made impossible. Any tolerance of illegal occupation on the part of the council undermines fairness. Social housing must be given to the most needy and it takes time and means testing and many forms and documented proof to discern exactly who this is. In the meanwhile, people can't just take what they please.

Social housing has to move with the times. As soon as decampment here is complete, a better estate can begin to be constructed: Homes of the Future. Though once afforded to these same bricks, this is a mantle which must necessarily be passed on.

Appearances can be deceptive and Woodberry Down's guards mustn't think that the ugly empty years now beginning for this estate are unjust or that squatting here is in any way acceptable. Both in its heyday, with its own school and shops, with its precise science of space allotment and a tang of newness in the air, and now, its hulking blocks incrementally shut, its windows broken one by one to the take the bracings, far uglier than ever expected, unmanageably large and predisposed to structural flaws, Woodberry Down embodies fairness.

Its guards circle in their slow-moving van, their headlights pushing back the dark, conscientious and informed.

Mike, who chose not to finish his GCSEs, is neither of these things. Once, not so long ago, as his grandmother and her friends had in fact recounted, there'd been no safety net. The poor had starved; they'd died of cold. Now their life opportunities and chances to become responsible worker citizens are given much greater consideration. Even their windows are of a minimum size. Eventually they will hit on just the right architectural design and prevent people feeling the way Mike does; evolution moves towards better things. Until that time though, Mike will probably keep on robbing.

Tonight he's taken an iPod, an Acer laptop, a *Moto Razr*, thirty quid, a quarter of top bud and no alarm has even sounded. Young people have so much more that's worth nicking now. Ten years ago, when Mike first got into the business, only old people were worth doing and they have alarms. Young people aren't as scared and tend to live in places with single-glazed windows. These days they've usually got even more than old people. If Mike's honest, he likes the feeling of burglary. Not only is it exciting but he gets a sense of righteousness from it. He's never imagined the world in quite the way John Saunders does but, strangely enough, it's a feeling of doing just what he was meant to do.

He is now sitting at home – in a flat in Finsbury Park not dissimilar to that occupied by Bernado and Hannah, though Mike's was awarded to him fairly. He's kept the iPod but he's swapped the rest for an oblivion Hannah would wax lyrical over. His eyes are closed and he's lying on the floor.

The knock is tiny. The voice a whisper. '…hello?'

Hannah and Bernado stand up. Beneath the door's already paling line, a torch beam sways.

'Hello? Yes?' Hannah answers clearly.

There is silence.

'Hello? Who are you?' Bernado calls. Glancing through the doorway into the main darkened living room, another torch beam plays over the balcony windows' tall metal. Frank and Leroy have taken position, as trained.

'I can't hear you... can you open the door...?' Frank's voice responds.

Anarchy, Douglas Johnson often used to tell his pupils, is comparable to the fizzing white screen of dots that's sandwiched between each TV channel change. Although in its brevity it might seem a refreshing contrast to the high resolution nausea of the real programme, it's a state which is untenable for any length of time. Hierarchies spring to fill the space like another episode of *Star Trek*. But wouldn't it be interesting, he'd asked, posing the line of inquiry to each ascending year he'd tutored – would it not be worth examining those airwaves devoid of content? Was it not a worthy question? To see what might exist in the gap between.

In the halflight now, Douglas's eyelids are gently closed over the fizzing white pixels of his thoughts. The trouble was, it was very difficult to unplug a person – both the broadcaster without and the hardware within were designed to make it problematic. Left unprogrammed or disconnected for any length of time, coherent patterns began to form themselves nevertheless, like ghosts inside the storm.

'Mercantile Imperialism: when Britain gained control of international trade by colonisation...'

Canary Wharf is the *Marie Celeste*, the breathing of a hundred PCs while outside unwatched sunlight towers grow long across the ground. Dawn is timed even on Sunday. Clocks with synchronised faces propel the seconds round in silence.

Ellipse Systems – unmanned but for Lol and his grandmother porn. A paunch broad enough to rest five magazines on.

Above, the teeth and fingers of the Docklands creation, cranes in stillness like mother birds feeding their young. *Own The Beauty* the sign here still reads, visible though Lol is sleeping, through the window across the Westferry road. Now, on Sunday morning, the conveyor only of solitary taxis, fully employed men almost dozing in their leather upholstery fumes, finally going home. *Own The Beauty* – a swift passing. Its rendered figures pause, walking, standing on their balconies, sitting on the great curving arcs of low steps: the only residents to see this sector's dawn. Their blue sky is a pallid reflection – ten foot by seven – of the heavens that are opening to release the last of summer onto this, the real world. Paradise. A paradise on Sunday.

On other continents, in countries where the dawn is ushered in by the sound of falling mortars and not the tones of the BBC, it might still seem in a very real way as if the world is ending. But here in the West, here in London where the sun unpackages itself between the buildings to fill with radiance abandoned polystyrene kebab boxes, to ignite the crystal droplets that hang in endless potential on the sides of the giant red BP smoothie, here on Junction Road the word apocalypse sleeps beneath unseasonable warmth.

'The Imperialism of Free Trade: when Britain dominated through its consequent ability to produce more goods more cheaply...'

Once Douglas Johnson's jacket had been a perfect tweed facsimile of the aspirations his father had attempted to imbue. Only over the course of a thousand bell-measured lessons had its itching label lumbered him with a caricature's rubbing gesture and eventually bestowed on him the nickname Flaky. Now slightly sick-stained down its left lapel and fraying, it has relented to a degree of comfort for Doug, who uses its pockets to store pieces of string and other interesting things he finds, like last week: a high voltage transformer.

At points in his career Douglas Johnson had wondered, despite a fairly in-depth knowledge of his chosen subject, exactly how it was that British history had conspired to morph such a deeply rooted class system into this, the modern world of meritocracy that was maturing in front of him term by term. By the year 2000 all his pupils owned mobile phones and could themselves have written fact-sheets on new-media career options. It was a progressively invasive crop of new expressions that flowered above the same old uniforms.

Childhood learning is drawn in lines. The written word, the numerical sequence, the nit comb and the picking of PE teams. Lines are the roads of knowledge. Year upon year, Doug had asked his classes to arrange their chairs in a circle around the outside of the room. Staring at each other across the embedded ranks of desk surfaces, they'd waited unfailingly for further instruction: fidget fingers, smirks, unconfident mouths.

'This,' Douglas had begun in his most expansive tone, 'is your nation. This is your blank screen. From this moment onwards, in order to attempt to replicate the conditions of anarchy, I will be issuing no further rules but this: an island in anarchy has no access to international travel, so none of you may leave.

'Now, you can do whatever you want.'

Protracted silence, in his final year as it had been every year before. Douglas had sat on his desk, his hands folded neatly beneath the soft beard, eyes sewing the pupils together.

A ratio of silence, equally degreed. Between their half-formed looks, the eyes of Betty Pullman had remained silently attentive, white shirt crisp over sentinel breasts.

One slim hand slowrising.

'Why have you got your hand up, Matthew?'

'Like whatever you want?'

'You don't need to raise your hand in an environment where there are no rules in force.'

Doug had glanced at the metallic, rotating spines of his watch.

Within fifteen minutes Mr Johnson's very last 9C had voted to abolish swearing. In twenty five, they'd begun to elect themselves a council on the basis of short-term tenures. They came to believe that it would be unfair for any representative to serve more than three terms. It was a double lesson and by half past eleven that morning they were in the process of designating a punishment scale, which they found difficult within the blandness of the classroom environment. As the bell had rung they'd looked up with surprise and disappointment, Betty Pullman still fingering her fifteen centimetre ruler. Several of them had wanted to stay through lunch.

And what had existed in the momentary space between? Rustling dissatisfied feet, embarrassment. He'd seen it slowly confirmed before his eyes, sadness mushrooming as he'd observed them – the truth was, anarchy left them purposeless. How it fell from their faces like a slipping rag as he lent forward, searching their expressions for clinging remnants.

Fighting for places as individuals with their defiantly styled ties – some years very short, others fat – they only added their own dynamic commitment to the rule of order by ploughing their roles into it. The truth was they loved the system. The love was very deep, much easier than the one they had for themselves.

And gradually it had come to Doug – his ten minute bicycle journey evolving into a new, slow panorama of chrome – that perhaps the lessons his father had so devoutly inflicted in the little cupboard underneath the stairs were not, as he'd always assumed, an abnormality or perversion peculiar to Mr Johnson Senior. Although Douglas's own failure to absorb the education was evident, he began to see that his father's teachings might in some way have existed on a far broader and more successful scale.

Now the history Douglas tried to understand and impart recurs in wreckage, drifting through the seas of an uncharted sleep, which laps a little further each day across his tastebuds.

'Capitalist Imperialism: when Britain invested directly in the sourcing and production of minerals, necessitating colonies once again.'

At **06:21** Stan wakes in the dawn light to see Doug and Davey sleeping peacefully on the bench beside him. His blankets are greasy with dew and night cold, adhered to his clothes, his bones ache and above him this Sunday is splayed unhindered through the sky. He looks at the remit of his life, this two foot margin of stolen charity shop bedclothes spread out either side of his legs, these paving stones and this abandoned Abbey National wall, and he begins to cry. The tears run out of his sleep encrusted eyes as silently as the daylight enters this city. Dislocated, loving the world, in some way that he's never loved it before.

You can't help but be impressed with the utter cohesion, the way no single fragment seems unnecessary. Genetics, a multitude of strands defying numerals. A society functioning on a plane unrecognisable to any of it its member-parts. Doug stands and hails buses all day long in the wrong place, screaming, but what's more brilliantly conceived than a system of bus stops and junctions and roads?

Genetics is a subject of particular interest to Doug these days, and not only for the lucky happenstance of its first letter. Genetics holds the meaning of life. The solution to each and every dichotomy of the human soul, awaiting nothing but translation. It's genetics that's birthed every market.

SALE, say the signs in the hardware shop and in the gift shop next door and the pet shop, in the Co-op; SALE they say, a latticework of understanding to filter in through your Sunday strolling thoughts, a rope bridge just an inch beneath your consciousness.

Betty Pullman must have had perfect genes nestled somewhere in their tiny writhing chains beneath her flesh; chromosomatic symmetry had formed ideals to flower in her fingernails and nipples. Her ankles: sacred curves. The biological swamp of her pupils. Genes for access development.

What does she look like now? Doug sometimes wonders. All our futures, plotted in spirals that we can't wrest out from under our skin. Betty gave him the photograph. He never would have asked for it from her. She stood in the halfwritten light of the form room after registration, between the grating desks. She stood and called him Sir with an arch in her voice set to shake off any form of sincerity. Blouse and shirt and tie, little navy blue skirt.

She said, 'I have something for you, Sir.'

All the innocence of childhood remembered, radiating from her, and in her eyes the swimming uknowables of corruption.

'OK Betty.' But he'd known. He'd felt it coming; she'd reached into her little satchel bag. Doug clearly remembers how Betty's fingers worked at the catch and how she glanced up at him, daring him to make her stop.

But he hadn't known. Had he known? What was the value in it for her? A washed-up secondary school history teacher with ketone breath. Unless she found evil sexy. Found sexy the exercise of power over him.

She handed it to him face down and left the form room, new landscapes promised in those breasts. He remembers the stage whisper of the door.

In the photograph she had been sitting with her legs spread into the shape of the letter M. This could be part of the reason why M is not the letter that Douglas Johnson has spent his subsequent life examining. A beautiful M with darkness at its tiny centre. Terrible things begin with M. Take madness.

And outside the tarmac yard had been scourged by a winter light so mean that it denied all detail. Only the most generic shapes: tree, ground, sky. A light to press against your soul. Of course he had reached to flick the fluorescents' switch. Just a tip of the chair, a touch of one fingertip. That didn't mean he hadn't intended to deliver the photograph straight to the Head. Had she taken others? Distributed them widely?

And it wasn't the M, with its clandestine messages, shiny unscented pheromones and frustratingly placed reflection. Nor was it the pale parted lips, the blonde hair that she'd sidled over one shoulder into view. It was the white shirt and badged tie. The flip-lifted navy skirt.

It was the uniform she wore that had sent back mycelium veins into his past.

And when the door had reopened and Douglas had raised his gaze, expecting to see that magnificent blonde face again but looking instead upon the visage of Mrs. Glap, head of the history department, it had occurred to him with a kind of bass-note finality that resistance might indeed be futile.

Douglas had sat alone that night in front of the television. His hair had been receding already, its shores drawing back to leave one small final island, the screen's irregular shadows shining on his scalp. Holding the remote control in one hand, he'd composed resignation letters on crumb spotted looseleaf paper, flicking ceaselessly back and forward between the news and the news and the news.

Hannah and Bernado stand now in the neglected corridor of their new flat. From outside, softly funnelled by the rim of his hat towards the letterbox, the security guard's breathing is clear.

'Why don't you just open the door and then we can talk to each other…?' he says.

'I can hear you quite clearly,' Hannah tells him.

'…what? I'm sorry…?'

'We can hear you,' Bernado answers loudly.

After this there's quiet: forty five seconds, more.

Retreating footsteps.

Beckoning her, Bernado moves into one of the bare rooms that might or might not become a bedroom soon. Through the broken window and the Sitex here, the dialogue is audible. The two figures – seen through tiny holes – are hard to watch. In the early daylight of the courtyard, they're standing beside the van's open door. Their uniforms are black with yellow trim.

'...They haven't been in there for more than a few hours; the door is changed since last night.'

'Definitely since last night.'

'How many d'you think? I only heard two.'

'I didn't hear any more than two.'

Hannah touches Bernado's wrist and shows him the beautiful blue clock face that glows on her mobile phone screen: **06:24**. People will be up soon. The guards have very little time before they must notify their superiors that they have failed.

Hannah is not the girl from the photograph that ruined Douglas Johnson's life; every place that Betty was bald, Hannah sprouts unshaven. Where Betty was born a leader, Hannah has yet to find a role in life. She cannot settle. She cannot believe in success. She had once dreamt of being an artist, working with dog shit and horse hair maybe. She's considered joining the Hare Krishna or maybe leaving for India where she'll find herself a cave and a juniper tree, but it can be quite difficult even in this age of low cost airfares to accumulate the necessary moneys for escape. So it is that she wanders from bottle to needle, asking questions like 'why not?' – which will never take her anywhere but deep space.

It might be tempting to see the guards' retreat as a point scored for them. They've caved into their van seats, first one then the other, and driven away into the morning light. **06:26**. Perhaps it's too late for any action but informing their superiors now.

'What you think?' Bernado asks her quietly as they survey the forecourt, shadows shrinking even as they watch. The bricks of Woodberry Down are infused with beauty as the blue sky begins to make itself known. A barking dog. The rattle of somewhere-dishes. The grasp of a distant engine moving on.

'When d'you have to go?'

He shrugs. 'Fifteen minutes.' And the concern on his face must be her guardian now, for Bernado works at a market stall flogging fake Halal meat on Dalston Lane each Sunday and that's life. 'Just keep the doors locked.'

'I can sleep I think.'

'I think you can sleep.'

'Ok.'

She watches him remove his many anklets and bracelets and place them carefully in an envelope which he stores in the front pocket of the tool bag. She sees him pull his wild hair back into a taut ponytail and from the underside of this same toolbag, remove a folded white shirt and black trousers. In the space clear of glass he proceeds to strip: tie-dyes and combat trousers in a little heap, softwood limbs in weakening shadow. The person who emerges, like *Superman*, is almost unrecognisable and Hannah's smile is bitter in the semidark of the squatted flat. After all they're only accessories.

John Saunders shifts slightly with the first ribbon of wakefulness, a moment that always occurs precisely three minutes before the alarm on the Teasmade sounds – maybe in some genetic hangover from times of danger and death. He hears the first kiss of its tiny heating system. He rolls over, sees the digitized numbers reading **06:27**. His first port of call today is the case of Stanley and Claire (deceased) Parsons. He knows only by the taste in his mouth that their file will see changes before night comes again. Waiting for gentle boiling noises, he lies comfortable in the knowledge that he is good because he's working on a day when others are at rest.

He will dress in a rhythm which has its own beauty; its own symmetry and perfect lines. His shirt is ironed, it slips like dandelion seed across his shoulders, over his widening load. His boots sit as close, as dark as adjoining cemetery plots beside the glosswhite skirting – socks laid over them. These little things are the components of happiness. Fulfillment is a pattern in the soul.

Indeed who is to say that Mike's addiction is his own fault, maybe his synapses were always blessed with tiny crack adaptors, ready, waiting for the moment when they would find their use. He wakes sweating, no need for alarm clocks when mortar bombs are falling in your mind.

And in the ash-saddled gloom of the Rose and Garter, Beryl Riley is uncoiling the Hoover's great tongue for its daily toil. Chris's sixty-nine-year-old mother completes the cleaning before eight every morning when her daughter and son-in-law rise. At **06:31** she can draw a tot from every optic and downs them with an inch of coke from the same glass. By nine she'll be asleep in the laundry room, where the scent of Daz hangs between the oxygen molecules, though there's never any laundry done there but her own brand of self-cleaning through sleep.

The Hoover screams its life.

The fag ends disappear.

On the third floor, Chris Saunders (née Riley) lies in sleep with her arm around her husband's gut.

He is dreaming. In Ken's dreams, a string of girls not unlike Betty Pullman give him ATMs without the need for antibiotics.

The Fetishisation Of Our Children had been Douglas Johnson's very last attempt to reconcile his thoughts about the world. Though now 25/26ths of all knowledge are out of bounds for Doug, in the nine months following his resignation he'd applied himself zealously to what had been a broadly faceted and groundbreaking work. Through its labyrinthine sentences and clever sub-textual connections, he'd harboured fantasies of a poetic justice that might right the scales with his literary success.

Hour after hour, diminishing hairline lowered over his papers, he chased the threads of his beliefs: the symbolism of the school tie, the sexuality of sameness, the unending chain of self-flagellation and dominion. Sometimes he seemed only one sentence from the answer, panting, frantic, in the dimness of his studio flat, offering up in altruism to the pool of human knowledge those oh so private details of his past. Sometimes it felt like he might conquer. But when the manuscripts had returned in their stamped, self-addressed brown envelopes and Doug had plucked them one by one from the hallway floor, the publishers' accompanying letters had featured a blank box where his name ought to have been and Mr Johnson Junior's retreat had begun in earnest. Opening the flap of the letterbox instead of the door, he had looked out at passing buses, imagining travelling to the curving edge of the world – and falling off it. Falling off it and finally being free.

It isn't his fault that he gets a hard-on at the thought of screwing schoolgirls – or of being a schoolgirl himself and getting screwed. Conformity, as Douglas had penned in his own concluding paragraph, lies like the seed of the next generation, deep inside us all. It was just that, strangely, the more you fought it, the more helplessly prominent it became. The twist within Douglas, that has divested his life of sanity, remains a direct result of disobeying the rules which had once determined what was best for him.

John Saunders uses the remote control button to release the autolocks on his little car. He loves the sound of his own heels in the unwoken road. No birdshit on his windscreen today.

On the Garter's first floor, John, Dave and John are waking to the sound of six hundred and fifty bottles falling simultaneously from their recycling container into the jaws of a purpose-built truck.

06:47.

144

Bernado is cycling dutifully towards Dalston. He has been hired by Dominic, a large white carcass of a man with nailbrush grey hair and one silver earring, not extravagant enough to waste tones of voice. Dom has hired Bernado because although he's Brazilian, when dressed smartly he can pass for a young Muslim. The stall, which Bernado runs alone for most of the day, feeling sick like a bad daytime soap actor, has low overheads and turns a high profit margin, the greatest expense from what Bernado can make out are the labels, which are printed on the Kingsland Road. Dom pays him a fiver an hour, cash in hand at four each day – since Bernado's visa expired he's had trouble making commitments on any kind of solid, legal or long-term basis.

He doesn't like leaving her there alone. He's had experiences. Five years squatting Britain's capital city now and it's so easy, like a game designed on the model of real life. There's always the police – here they're honest. But still he has had experiences. There are landlords who are crazy. Crazy's indigenous every country. There are times when you're boarded in. And for a few years now he's been hearing the same mentality washing around with those he meets, council properties are safe, council properties are guaranteed, they've got to do things by the book. It has been one of Bernado's experiences that when you start to hear a loophole spoken of generally, the authorities have usually heard of it too.

John Saunders' Golf has a polarised strip across the zenith of every sliding view. Anything that happens fifteen foot or more above the pavement happens in aquamarine. The early sun is a jellyfish, the blue clouds pass across a bluer sky.

He indicates right from Parliament Hill into the Holly Lodge estate, the very first of Britain's council house developments. A giant toyland of faux Tudor, lawns, leaning pines and community notice boards. The flats are worth a packet here now. The last council tenants sit behind their net curtains, feeling the infringement of a crawling sensation that reaches them with the distant sound of hedge-trimmers.

First, as quietly as though carried by conveyor belt, he drives between the great six storey blocks, their balconies and painted beamwork. Another right, a left. To indicate brings the greatest pleasure when there's no other vehicle on the road. Past Oakshott Avenue. Two more turns. The estate makes him think of *The Prisoner*. John amuses himself by glancing in the rear-view mirror and envisaging a giant white destructive balloon. It's the sort of place that he himself would like to retire to. He imagines each and every one of the neighbours engaged in a united community effort of noise reduction.

Stanley stands and his limbs are painful like he's been homeless for five years. He doesn't glance towards the breakfast skip now but only gazes, glazes past the bench his new friends share as a bed. Vorley Road lies there, a fingernail of the sun's rays inched around its sign.

He is free.

Perhaps alarm clocks are sounding in HMP Pentonville, the tail of August filtering through the heavy wired glass and bars, while buses carry babysitters,

146

groundworkers, all the Sunday people to their out of rhythm roles, pausing for pickup just outside the prison's gates. The trees there are limbless and leafless; pillars of sanity. Maybe there were once reports commissioned to inform all coppicing decisions, with no exceptions made for the views of inmates. Past their feet the buses slide. A nation granting such vending machine smoothness isn't built on unfounded choice.

Stanley thinks about the word 'free' and its many connotations. Costing nothing, valueless, or unrestrained. But it gains meaning like a magnet, lifting the strings of people's hearts, the sensations too basic to have names for.

Stanley has no change, no tiny five pence pieces too light to hold tangible value, nor any pound coins with their comforting thickness, their tangy little embossed symbols, for England or Scotland or Wales. But an idea has begun to surface inevitably, maybe heralded by the advert slickness of his smoothie dream.

He could go home. He could get the car – and he could sell it.

The free market, he thinks. And with this prospect an inundating sadness comes.

Perhaps he's only lonely. He pictures the tiny touches of Claire's life's work, dotted at roadsides, train stations and in shopping precincts, facilitating interconnectivity fingers. He wants to make a sentence, or a sign maybe, a sound, something that could hold the sense of disassembly that's made such inroads into him.

He could sell the car and he could buy himself a meal.

The idea germinates, irrepressible.

DC Saunders pulls to a halt between a badly-parked metallic olive Ka and a well-parked Audi and he relieves the ignition key. Sits in the unique silence of an agreeable city district on a Sunday, morningtime, a peculiarly human kind of beauty. He doesn't smoke and enjoys this while he waits.

He has no reason for sitting and waiting here except for the reason that this is the very last time he would be. And this is reason enough. He must think himself into Mr Parsons' place and at this time of day his thoughts are unconstricted by reality – by personality. He could be anyone. He could be Stan.

The Parsons' home sits in the shade of its own quarantine, sucked shut between the roses. A warning to these constantly parenting, dinnerpartying neighbours – a warning made of stains and bars and suddenness.

John Saunders breathes deeply, extends his gaze over the street. The dew is a careful embrace, the stalks of daisies, the dampness of brick. There goes the shadow of a gull, or a pigeon, unreprised. Could it be possible, he unwinds his window – could it be possible that in the secret softness of the morning he can hear a woman pee? A splash of liquid on enamel, as delicate a wakeful noise as the world will ever hear. Breathing deeply, he views both of this avenue's exits; one before him, one in the triad of his mirrors. Stanley Parsons walked down one, there is no other way to leave. He walked down one with the unfettered ease of a man who doesn't understand the paperwork it will create for others.

As John Saunders leans his nape against the velour head rest, sparing a spontaneous flick of thought for the sagging tits his brother's wife must surely be condemned to by now, and remarking to himself simultaneously on how blue polarised glass can really be, Stanley Parsons emerges from the Swain's Lane exit.

A little grey leper without a bell, he looks at the house, which has been placed inside the safe of its own walls.

John imagines – just tweaking her nipple, just a little bit. Blue as the corona of the Mediterranean sea. Blue leaves motionless above the windshield. Just sticking his cock between them, just the once. It's such a beautiful peaceful dawn for masturbating in public. Just sticking his cock into her foul-mouth piss-blonde face. John invites the images of every curtained window in as his palm slides like wet heaven into his fly, hollyhocks nodding beside the lawns, the doorbells, all the number plaques and the sleeping men and women. Just fucking her and fucking her while she chews the edges round her nails, the way she does sometimes when she watches TV. He gazes from the white painted door of number fifty four to the two full milk bottles sitting in front of fifty six, his frenzied fist jerking in his lap as the morning fills each gracefully reflective windowpane, all looking down on him. Her wrinkled pursed lips sucking him, all dry and bitter sewer words, his foreskin tingling hot, his cum uprising. His eyes pause at the bright pink tricycle lying sideways on the lawn of fifty eight, trying to shift on quickly for fear of ejaculating while it's in his view, but too late he sees Chris's little brown arse stretched open for him... to spill like warm sadness, into his hand. To go cold inside his trousers while he breathes and looks up and sees the blue, a tricycle emblazoned like the memory of the sun.

The throbbing resonance of childhood jealousy. The slow remembrance – of who he is today, right now. In his lap his penis is deflating. He watches it as a man might watch his past receding, a tug, a loss, nostalgia, the real world. As he begins to close his fly, he looks directly through the windscreen and sees Stan's figure, a shocked equation on the little crazy-paving garden path.

John Saunders opens his mouth. And both hands fumble with the zip.

He abandons it and grabs the Golf's doorhandle.

Stanley Parsons had walked up Vorley Road, where he'd once carried Co-op bags himself, doubled up for wine and milk. The sunrise was in the trees. His hands made little brushing sounds with every step he took.

Claire must have seen this time of day more often, she must have stood alone in their living room sometimes, seeing trees like these, or winter trees, and wondering what access development meant for people, what her life was really for. Had she looked down on Stanley, just ever so slightly, for succeeding in a field which did not succeed itself? Even once she had finally realised the extent of what Strategy Solutions gave to the world. What had she thought about, looking out at this city in her own morning, fifty years old, council tenancies winking out around her like candleflames? It was access development that drew us all into one – six billion of us, more incredible with every passing instant of our lives.

Genetics, the great unspecified reason. An amalgam of unfailing predispositions, veering, dancing and reacting, creating the concepts both of fairness and of freedom and setting one against the other in an endless motion of advancement. The world wasn't ending. Not even in that moment of the TV's crescendo when it had felt to Stan like it might be; the world wasn't ending at all. In fact, no one knew how long it might go on like this.

Highgate Cemetery was a Jurassic sprawl of graves and undergrowth; Stan looked in between the railings as he passed. They must cremate ninety per cent of the bodies, or some massive portion, or surely every verge would be planted with corpses by now.

The tallest of Holly Lodge's peaks revealed through the trees, Stanley thought about envelopes he'd had, in files from 1974. His name and this address, handwritten in a style that you don't see often anymore, stiff loops and crocheted letters. He thought about the way that they had burned as he walked into the Holly Lodge estate and looked towards his home.

His walking terminated. They'd boarded up the two storey semi-detached in which he and Claire had carefully amassed their lives. Purpose-made screens, metal girders. Their blue Rover stood in front of a derelict, exhausted rings of soot around its steel front door and its unanimous broken windowholes. The viticella had been flowering and there was glass all over the path.

Stan has no access to the Rover's service history in its little vinyl envelope, to the MOT certificate or to the keys.

And what is the car worth to him, immobile like this, if he cannot prove it's his?

What does it even mean to own something without proof?

Nothing more than a statement to himself or to the world, he realises: I own this car.

In the unearthly quiet of Highgate's Sunday morning, Stanley gazes at all the things he has no right to; the world's previous collusion in his existence. And his spirit makes a little popping sound not dissimilar to the initial crackle of Les Dennis' voice midway through the question on well-known wines. A snap, a crackle and a pop.

It was the pasty pixel carving of Les' features. Each excess and career failure etched in electronic flesh, talking, as if there was no end to the words he had ready to unleash upon his million teledistant lovers.

It was the advert break. The voice of a million essential services. It was authentic Malay prawn laksa. If you need a low cost loan at your convenience. This is not just food. And the easing music and the open world of the car in front is a Toyota. It was the advert break.

Stanley was standing with a towel in each hand and both were dirty and he didn't know where to put them down, because to put them down was to make that surface dirty when he was trying to clean, to improve the situation, so he was just standing there, completely and totally unable to act.

The vastness of the world flooding in towards him. He remembered seeing an Asian woman interviewed after the tsunami, jabbering about the rising sea and about her endless dreams.

All he could see was Les Dennis. The stuff didn't stop coming from Claire's mouth. He had no newspaper on which to put the towels down. To get newspaper he would have to put them on the carpet, the sofa, the edge of the rented hospital bed. How many people were watching Les right now? They only ever counted viewing figures in the millions. At least a million people. What did a million people look like if they stood next to each other? He remembered seeing that Asian woman and the sealight in her eyes. He had no newspaper.

He wanted to call someone but he was only meant to call once she was dead. There was the telephone, a cordless, neat, sweet and complete on the sideboard between the get well cards, here were the lever-arch files on the dining room table with their plastic sleeves ready hole-stamped and their lists of numbers, schedules, medications, records. Who could he call? There was a difference between an emergency and something no one could do anything about and this was the difference, this useless silver cordless telephone. This sense of total isolation. One tiny island, one cartoon hump rising out from the ocean unending, one droop-curve palm; this is death. And the rest of the world went on; Les Dennis talked. The rest of the world went on unchanged. He had read outs and dials and some made beeping noises that were meant to transcend language, intelligible even to the home-user, but he had no idea what to do now Claire was haemorrhaging. It wasn't vomit because her body was not the force behind its expulsion. It issued from her, black almost green and at tremendous volume, without the slightest movement of her muscles. He'd been trying to change her urine bag but after he'd removed the full one, the tube protruding from the dressing on her lower belly discharged, whatever black stuff was inside her it was everywhere, disregarding the barriers of organ integrity like they were nothing more than coloured lines on a map.

He would have to bend over Claire to change the towel under her head next and the expulsion coming from her was growing, haemorrhage was the word without question. The nurses, the visiting doctors had not described this possibility. It was conceivable that the haemorrhaging might become explosive if she didn't die quickly enough.

And he, not even he but they, everybody, every recourse within the methodical management of Claire's deterioration – not he but *it*, the national health system – was not allowed; they were not allowed to intervene. To do anything but watch her die that way.

A pop.

The opening thud of a car door.

Stanley turns to see a man running towards him from a distance of fifty metres or so – a flushed pellet winging its way past the parked cars, and he makes the shape of an O with his mouth.

Holding his trousers up with one hand and fixating a bullgaze on Stan, the man is obviously crazy. The man is obviously crazy and obviously a member of the police force. Stanley tears one last strung glance from the homestead that he and Claire had occupied until their lives took such unexpected turns. He arcs into a cartoon bounce that impels him, running speed without the need for acceleration.

And so the strands of this story begin to come full circle. Stanley Parsons can't exist without food or safety and every thread of life around him, engineered by unconscious Goethean purpose, meshes to create a world in which food and safety can't be gained when you cease to take part.

So Stanley runs from the law, runs as though the wind will carry him out of his own genes and into some heaven of freedom and fairness made one, runs beneath the billboards and between the wall-tight houses – runs and asks himself just exactly what has led him here.

'Can't we give her something, something to make it easier... can't we give her more morphine?' he had begged.

But the doctor had explained with diligence that they'd done everything they could – and all that was left was to watch the cancer win.

A blind aggregate species.

Stanley runs.

He is not dead. His legs pump ferocious fuel from a body he has starved for days. He is most definitely not dead. Although he's been not dead for quite a while now, as he hurtles away from the place he'd once unthinkingly called home, it's the first time he's really understood the feeling.

When it had become obvious that Claire's cancer was terminal, and when that obviousness had been confirmed by the doctor's decisions, when death had first really entered the Parsons' lives, that was when Stanley had begun to become not dead, a condition which only existed in its palpable contrast to Claire. You stepped through a hole in the curtains when death was in the house.

Everything was more in focus, not metaphorically but literally, dark was darker and colours held these secrets. Because you were afraid, you were constantly afraid when someone was dying near you – this was the awareness of being wholly unprotected.

At first there had been extensive smooth-tiled nights of waiting in the hospitals, the punctuation of the dashing journeys, always needing to be where you weren't, and all this was surreal – a hidden carnival of panic beneath the map of a city you thought you knew – but it was also a current, to carry you away.

With the decision, things had changed. When Claire had come home for good, that was when the condition of being not dead had really become Stan's world. A place of thick slow-moving strangeness, here normal things looked abnormal: the supermarket that you still needed to visit, coming home to a very different front door. Or the biscuit tin, which had never seemed so vivid as it had that evening beside the kitchen windowsill: a thing made out of matter and in some way a beautiful thing.

Stanley had inhabited this shadow version of the real world side by side with normal people for about two weeks and when, in Claire's death agonies, he'd begun to notice the sound of the television, which had been so very constant, suddenly changing – its many voices seeming to draw together and combine into one massive semi-metal hum – it was true that he'd wanted it to explode. He had willed Les Dennis, who'd looked out at him as though across an infinite plane of sadness, to let it all end.

But now as Stanley sprints across the stretches of public lawn, as he leaps and runs like lace over the pavements, not being dead is a fizzing in his veins. Now he wonders at that moment, before the fire engines came to douse the night with blue, he wonders if what he felt in front of Claire's body might in some way have been an extraordinary or dangerous thing.

Yes he's not dead. He's really sure of it now. He could be dead at any moment but he is burningly not and the feeling of it carries him away.

Beneath a sign offering **FANTASTIC APARTMENTS**.

Beneath one that asks him thoughtfully: **WORKING TOO HARD TO FIND A PLACE TO BUY? WE'LL MAKE IT EASIER FOR YOU WITH NEW TEXT PROPERTY ALERTS!**

Between the few early pedestrians, Stan Parsons runs, along Junction Road's endless line.

Douglas and Davey still lie at rest as he reaches them.

Their skins have differing purple tones.

Doug leans his head on the younger man's shoulder, the shade of the small tree's branches falling across their lax faces. Stanley gazes on, but there is nowhere to hide. And back, one hundred metres further down the gradually warming road, DC John Saunders holds his trousers. He pursues.

'...*Douglas*...' Stanley says '...*Douglas*...'

157

Help, he thinks, the words spelled out in bed-sheets in his mind, chaotic letters six feet high, and the man's dark fingers jump in slumber around the bulge of his secreted carrier bag. It must have been a respite for him, just to sleep without caring, his lips are wet as his hand jerks and the bag drops without fanfare onto the pavement. His lips are wet as if on the point of murmuring words.

John Saunders' footsteps outpace the distance. And the contents of the bag slip out at Stan's feet – and he stands there.

A broad book with a dark green cover.

And one letter, in gold leaf, centrally set.

The letter G.

The Macmillan Family Encyclopaedia, Stanley reads, and he looks with a slight edge of incomprehension at what is resting on top: unexcitingly coloured and pragmatic. From the frayed plastic edge of the bag, tilted against the comprehensive collection of all G knowledge is the muzzle of a gun.

The great BP smoothie above Stanley echoes strawberry light into Junction Road. He sees the ruler clouds of leaving planes, tiny sketches, and in between the approach of sprinting shoes he hears the song of city birds.

For all those months Doug had owned a gun and for all the shouts and the dimness in his eyes, he'd never once drawn it. Stan wonders as he bends down whether God is in the encyclopaedia.

The flutters of the plastic carrier bag echo leaves.

God is in the encyclopaedia.

On pages 217-219, slightly flood-damaged and smelling of off-milk. 'Is the notion of God, which correlates so closely with the self-understanding of humankind, merely a projection of humanity's self-consciousness onto an unresponding cosmos?' it asks.

But as Stan picks up the rather heavy gun the sense that he has is not in any way one of unresponsiveness. Thin palms, a fifty year old's skin, latticed with tiny diamonds. He sees the policeman cease to run and for the first time since the TV exploded, Stan feels as if he and the cosmos could actually be as one.

Davey was little more than a child when the Dunblane massacre happened, but he remembers exactly where he was. Revising for his GCSEs in his bedroom, with the TV on in the corner, they had interrupted *Columbo* halfway through.

He remembers watching the grey panning shots of the schoolyard, all the doors shut long after the horse had bolted, his fingers resting atop the buttons of his scientific calculator. He remembers his imagination wandering into the barrel of a gun – how the sight of the world must whiten to nothing with the blast.

Stanley doesn't remember Dunblane happening, where he was or what had occupied him on that day.

'Stanley Parsons,' DC Saunders says, just to make sure.

'Yes, that's right.'

A fly passes them and circles Davey's empty cider bottle, creating unseen patterns in the air.

'There's no need for you to have a gun– ' the police officer starts reasonably, 'that's ridiculous. Why not put it down and let's just go?'

Stanley doesn't answer him though – for a moment, thoughts are simply obstructed – his eyes open, his face as white as a satellite dish.

Once, when Stanley was on holiday with his wife and they drank iced coffees in pretty cafes in Lisbon's square, he'd seen while walking back to the hotel a homeless man with elephantitis, begging. The picture had stayed with him for years.

The man's face had engulfed itself, uncontained flesh swelling his head to perhaps four times its natural size. His left eye had still been discernible, squashed into the lower part of one cheek, sneaking glances out beneath the overhanging protuberances.

Stanley had tried to force himself to go up to the man and give him money; he'd felt a little guilty at how appalled and disgusted that face had made him feel. But his fear had been a stronger contender in the end.

He'd veered away from that sitting picture of wrongness before even drawing close. Just close enough for long enough to see the little badge on the tramp's right lapel, an old taxi driver's licence – staring out at the world through a completely normal photograph.

Stanley is afflicted as he looks at the officer – and around at the inert street – with an elongated and lonesome sense of déjà vu.

Not far away, Hannah sits in the continuing gloom, rolling herself a cigarette and searching in their bags for a match that isn't there.

Encircled by the first waking of North London's inhabitants, a barely sensory breeze of half-dreams and Radio 2 exuded from every building on every side, Stan Parsons and the policeman stand in opposition.

There is very little traffic on the road on a Sunday at **07:10**.

With self-consciousness Stan raises the gun, which is made – almost everywhere but the trigger – out of absolutely straight lines.

He lifts the straight nose and puts it against the side of his own head – the right hand side – and then they both stand still. The earth turns, for Stan perceptibly.

Not far off at all, though irrelevantly for him, Ken, John, Dave and John are putting on their watches, preparing themselves for a third and final expedition to Mike's front door.

Hannah hunts through every crevice, her hand brushing the brown envelope which is stashed down at the bottom of her bag, but there is no match. And outside, leaning casually against the low wall of the estate, taking in the sun, a smartly dressed man with a bluetooth earpiece is smoking an early Marlboro Light, delicate nicotine fumes washing in through the holes in the windows and caressing Hannah's nostrils with addiction.

Mike is splashing water onto his face in front of a rust-spotted mirror when the Merc parks outside, looking into the sink and bemoaning the flat's bad drainage. And as Hannah finally sticks the fag into her mouth and works the key with that hopeless sense of predestination that being a smoker so often brings, the man with the bluetooth raises his softly smiling eyes to take in London's sky.

The muzzle of the gun is cool.

Douglas makes a sleepy grunting snore, his empty fingers curling round the air and stirring. Beside him Davey is shifting too.

Stanley can't spare a glance for them as the first moments of the morning become visible before their blinking eyes. Convex expressions. Douglas stiffens and Davey's mouth falls softly ajar.

When the two Johns synchronise shoulders against their own handwriting on the wood, Mike raises his reflection in rhythm to the smashing noise: a shaven-headed, rather under-developed boy, wearing a look of fatal chagrin. He comes wet-necked from the bathroom to see John and John moving towards him. They each take hold of one arm, lift his dirty socks up from the floor. And as Hannah calls, the man, with the roll-up's unlit end protruding over the threshold of the doorway, moves towards her and instead of reaching into his trouser pocket for a Clipper, takes hold of both her arms, it might seem – to Stan, to her in fleeting seconds and probably to Mike as well – that the balance of the universe is a thing of utter irrevocability.

She tears herself out of his grip and dives backwards, trying to shut the door in his face, but from the left another smart white-shirted man has popped into existence and before she knows it he is attacking her as well. She falls down onto the hallway floor as they enter the flat, kicking at their faces as they chase to find an ankle-hold – their fingers enclosing despite all her efforts, dragging her with the ease of applying Tippex to paper, feet-first towards the door.

'Put the gun down and go,' Stan echoes, 'Why not.'

Pronouncing in his own fractional voice the great screaming monologue of evolution. The world isn't ending. If he thinks about fire and brimstone, it isn't any more than a metaphor.

Carried through the little passageway and out into the summer light where Ken Saunders stands waiting like the stern of a new vessel, Mike has one brief chance to appreciate how the contrasts slide and play across the turtle-waxed roof of the car. He is deposited into the back seat and there he sits between the thighs of greater men. The engine is rekindled as he looks out through the darkened glass and asks finally, 'Got any spliff for the road?'

Though Hannah battles, her struggles are weakened by years spent without visits to the gym: she catches glimpses of the faces between her own kicking motions and they are smiling at her. They deliver her out onto the tarmac, to lie like a fish under the summer sky, and they pull closed the door between her and Mike's slim savings – or to put it another way, between her and BA Flight 152.

No, the world was a perpetual motion machine. She said sometimes that people were trading on the edge of a volcano but the truth of the matter was, no matter how many times it got predicted, there just didn't seem to be any grounds to fear the apocalypse right now.

So where were we going then?

Stanley opened his mouth and verbalised the question – waiting for the policeman's suggestion.

'Just somewhere nice and quiet,' John Saunders says.

But if we weren't hitting an ending, surely we must have been on some path – there must have been a swathe of future out ahead. Was it no more than a random spill of multifarious happenings? An avalanche of them? No wonder we needed the government, and the sense of security gained from a private pension, and photograph albums full of meaningful moments and their meaningful linear chains, no wonder we needed chat shows to get together and compare and contrast our experiences of trying to stay in control of our lives. No the world wasn't ending. In fact there was no reason why we shouldn't always go on like this – happyrattling domino style into further years of mass sporting events, e-commerce, international debt and new crisp flavourings; there wasn't any reason why we shouldn't continue into further eons of possibility for access development; the future might most definitely be orange. We might keep dying but we'd keep living too, and make more of ourselves and more and more, and find more food for ourselves or design it, and so help the rest of the chain along as well until there was no stopping any of us. There was no reason why not at all.

As he'd thought walking down the path and out of the gate, little street and window stars amassing as the view before him,

why not?

The question wasn't *Why?* It never had been, but something far more frightening.

A theft had been going on around them, an invisible theft occurring on every side as he'd stood in their living room prohibited from altering the course of Claire's death, immobilised by a dummy question, a theft in every home around them.

This is what was taken – this unshelteredness – and look at what it means.

Stanley steps out from the pavement. He moves with moderate backward footsteps into the silence of the junction. John Saunders raises a hand to gesture 'stop' but Stan doesn't, continuing to reverse into the widest reach of the thoroughfare, his trouser cuffs dragging against the abrasive road.

Far from the car and its inbuilt two-way radio, Ken's brother's cheeks have begun to assume an enamel tint. His tongue touches each corner of his mouth and he glances at the surrounding storefronts, still inaccessible, at the open throats of the roads that conjoin to form this intersection.

Stanley stands with his back to all that asphalt.

In early July, Douglas had found the gun, wrapped up inside the strong greasy paper of a bag.

That bag itself lying in between the loose flowers of screwed up tabloids and freebie ads, Douglas might have looked from a distance like he was on an all time low – but as he'd unwrapped it and sat with its stolid shape between his palms, for the first time in a long time it hadn't been the weight of Douglas's own life upon his back. It seemed like insanity to protect an old carrier bag from the world, but it was nothing short of a Herculean task for Douglas Johnson to protect the world from his carrier bag.

With a cursory glace at the lettering, he had disposed of the pistol's oily wrapper, a neatly sized sackie with a clever plastic interior that had once held someone's pizza on a roll.

Indeed the trigger is decidedly greasy in the curl of Stan's index finger now.

Doug is looking with an expression of bereavement, first at Stan, then at the emptied carrier bag. With great care, one hand on Davey's slowly moving knee, he reaches down to retrieve his volume G.

Here comes the sound of an approaching vehicle.

It's a white transit van, making its lumbering way around the corner of the Holloway Road – and seeing Stanley in the centre of Archway's convergence, a few feet from the dotted white line, it slows. As it draws nearer, through the windscreen, Stanley's eyes meet a stranger's. The van judders. The handbrake can be heard.

It's a young man behind the wheel with what looks like a long marijuana cigarette in his mouth. Throwing searches, he locates the policeman's figure.

There must be protocols for things like this.

On Stanley's right, a double decker bus turns in from Vorley Road.

He watches it accelerate as the van stands idling before

him, watches it jolt and pull forward and finally halt just past the Give Way sign where Douglas Johnson and Davey Barnes are standing. It's a number 41. Doug is clutching Volume G once more, irresolute and landlocked as its doors slide open, bearing a look of infinite surprise.

Behind it, more are coming. A little Fiat with a rattling exhaust.

The newsagents that are open on Sunday are placing their billboards onto the paving stones in Tufnell Park and Kentish Town. The *Islington Gazette* reads: **Vampire Rapist Stalks North London**. The *Sunday Times* talks of climate change.

Between the switches of early morning channel surfing, drifting in through windows progressively – a dawn chorus of car horns. It's hard to find anything worth watching on a Sunday. Last night's *National Lottery Results* or an item about hardcore truancy on *BBC News 24*.

People eventually stand and wander over to their windowsills, in dressing gowns, with bowls of cereal or cups of instant coffee in their hands.

Hardcore truants are costing the economy eight hundred million pounds a year.

There are traffic problems outside today.

Mike and the men that are holding Mike draw to a sighing stop, the Mercedes' grill three feet away from the back of a Marks and Spencer lorry, and John and Dave crane their necks out of the car into the amiable summer air as they look for the cause of the problem.

Through the historic sepia tint of the passenger window though, Ken recognises his older brother from a distance. Ten yards from the centre of the standstill, underneath a striped café canopy, ostensibly at a loss and craftily trying to do up his fly.

When Bernado returns much later today and the roads are almost unobstructed, the Woodberry Down flat in which he left Hannah will be empty; re-bolted, the door once more removed and replaced by steel. And Hannah – who perhaps has been allowed to live under the misapprehension that some things in this world are free – will by then have had the truth firmly reinstated in her life.

It's not possession that forms nine tenths of the law for possession is an abstract concept. It is power, and no power is greater than that of the universal will.

Not long from now she will wander down the Holloway Road, intoxicated like a gyroscope. She will have stolen a bottle of Vladivar from the off-licence on the corner of the Seven Sisters Road, the Punjabi shopkeeper merely watching her sloping exit and marvelling at the undead children of twenty-first century western life. She will not think herself clever, particularly, but she will remember how very many off-licences there are in North London whose staff have never seen her face before. Not clever but capable of survival. Capable of getting for herself the things that she most needs.

Perhaps in reality she doesn't want a better future – though the call of a personally chosen rug or textured notebook, a window and view, a front door with its own key, are melodies infused with longing, indeterminate homesickness – there's a part of her, an ungovernable part, that hates them. Some great thinker, some monk or hermit from one ancient civilisation or another had once said, Hannah knew, the things you own will end up owning you.

So she owns nothing, not her clothes, her tobacco and skins, not the brown envelope that was close to containing enough. Hannah owns nothing and nothing owns her.

As she approaches the rear end of what seems to be one of the nastiest gridlocks the borough of Camden's ever seen, through the oily swill of potato-based alcohol she'll level her gaze on the multi coloured backs of a crowd and smile to herself at the fact that the world can still sometimes offer a surprise.

Drawing up to the crux of the throng, where the traffic's stuck as if in icing, she will be seen by a wide open face, from the back of a Mercedes. The windows lowered, and John and Dave half-obscuring his view, Mike will gaze out at her as the booze rocks her back and forward along the pavement.

He'll open his mouth to shout but won't go through with it. He'll look out past the neatly ironed shirt that graces Dave's barrel-chest and there, walking alone with her bottle, she'll be scot-free.

It would be hours.

Around him the traffic would pressurise into a rough hexagonal shape – from which he would jut, like the last forelock of Douglas Johnson's hair.

People exiting their vehicles, far back where they couldn't see the cause, standing in ones or twos amidst the detritus of a traffic flow, would begin to conjecture; discussing increasingly unlikely things.

All day car horns would rise dizzily towards the sky and SDP, as he'd sometimes used to refer to himself, would think about the feeling of being alive.

Sitting there at the thickened crossroads he would imagine this street, all the streets in which they lived, seen from above as the satellites surveyed them; the fields of aerial towers, roped in succession on Britain's flattest horizons. The shaded leafmould parks and many changing generations of brick. The routes, the signals. A garden of connection.

And the extraneous things, that seemed to grace the world without permission. Ferns growing in crevices under railway bridges or the objects, ghosts of their previous lives, that lie by fences and next to motorways.

The plastic bags, flying like flags, on the beanpoles of council allotments.

The truth of genetics seemed to lie all around him – society submerging them in it, arms awave as though hailing buses – all of them, like an anemone bed.

And Stanley sat embedded in the dark tar in the centre of the incident, the foundling pistol held against his head. One by one remembering the details of Claire's face as he listened to the horns continue, intolerable and lovely, he felt a profusion of solidarity – an undividedness.

How Loud It Is

The first thing I want to say is that this is not a story that goes anywhere in particular, by dint of the fact that I'm not really sure what it meant, this thing I want to tell you about.

For a start, he wasn't mad. Because when we say mad, we mean out of control and he wasn't that. I should say that I do know this guy. I've seen him around at least – he's one of those faces – so maybe not know him as such.

He was walking on East Street. I was drinking that morning so I had a lot of time to watch. I saw him; the first thing I thought was 'mad' and it took a while to realise that wasn't the case. We say 'mad' and I guess we mean a kind of spilling over, where what's happening inside is so heavy duty that we can't control how it looks to anybody else. But it wasn't that – he could've controlled himself. He just didn't care.

He had this long straggly ponytail and thick glasses,

clothes like a woodwork teacher wears. When I first started school it was called CDT in fact, which was Craft, Design and Technology – though by the time I finished it was D&T, so you can see what happened there. Anyway he was a skinny, shambly, quiet bloke. Looked like a lot of 1970s prog rock would be his cup of tea. Not the sort of person you'd look twice at. But first, he was walking incredibly slowly. So slow it took him literally ten minutes to get to the crossroads and out of my line of sight. And staring down at the pavement just in front of his feet. Creeping one foot forward in front of the other, the whole time shaking his head – not to say no to anything, but like he didn't understand.

I watched him go right the way down to the clock; I drank my Stella, and this is the thing he kept doing. This I saw him do four times. He'd stop, look up at the sky instead of down at his feet, and raise his arms up, like asking *Why?*

I swear he wasn't mad. It was one of those things you end up thinking about, because you can't find a category for it. It was half-day closing so there wasn't anyone else about. Everywhere closes on a half-day here still, Daisy's and the post office and the chemist and fuck anyone who needs a prescription.

It wasn't that long ago, early this summer, everything pretty bright in the street. People get their belief back when the summer comes. Even Munk gets happier. Sun takes the borders away. I was waiting for Kate to finish, keeping half an eye on the door she'd be coming out from. She takes her uniform off before leaving always, but it still takes her a while to get back to who she is without it, so if I'm not working we go somewhere. Because it was summer, we were going down the river.

To see someone look so sad when everyone else was thinking in the summer way...

I did tell Kate about him that day, but it was more the sort of thing that's come back since. I'm quite often thinking I might see him. If I'm in East Street especially, but all over town. It's not a big place after all.

'He wasn't mad,' I told her.

But she goes, 'I don't think you can ever tell.'

We sat there by the river all afternoon and evening. I took my other beers. That's the nature of my job though – sometimes I work Sundays. I'm with this company, which is really Jim and his wife and the van and me, moving people from one house to another. It's amazing how they always want the stuff set up the same way in their new place. I mean, you'll never get a couple who go 'Oh no, don't put it there, that looks just like the old house.' They want to recreate it exactly like what they just moved out of. They want it to be *better* but just the same. Like how you can go into pretty much any house in the world and it'll only take you two guesses at most to work out where an item's kept. That's ergonomics.

Katie'd had a good shift, twenty quid of tips. We were laughing about how they manage to make beer from a can taste so rough. Come the end, I mean not even the end but the last three inches, it's so flat it tastes like you opened it six weeks ago. Stella's gone downhill. It didn't used to taste like it does now. Once you've got the market buttoned, you're basically in the free and clear to start fucking over your customers.

She asks me if I've got any weed and I tease her for a bit but then I pass it over. The river is lovely by that part, wide and flat. We watch these two kids on the other side of the park chase each other and scream the new words for games that are probably just the same as the ones we used to play. She skins up and we sit and get stoned and watch the river caps change, endlessly change and never look like they're changing.

I start off by telling her about this guy, asking if she's seen him. She serves most people at one point or another. But she doesn't know who I mean and it's hard to describe what made it important.

I wanted to tell him like, mate, there isn't any answer and you might as well just sit down on the pavement if you're going to worry about it that much. But then I hadn't said anything.

Kate goes, 'Everyone here's fucking mad. You don't have to be mad to live here, but it helps.'

Since Olly's sister had gone to New Zealand, she'd been googling every place and talking about how much the tickets cost. But if people really want to leave, they do. Otherwise it can't be that bad. In New Zealand everyone's friendly apparently.

I could have been friendly to that guy that day, but he didn't look like he wanted anyone to be.

'I suppose there's different kinds of madness,' I said. But actually, I wasn't thinking that. I was thinking that he wasn't mad, it's just that I didn't want to repeat myself. I was thinking that, until I could find a way to store it, probably I wasn't going to be able to forget him. You don't see that many things here that are out of place.

The things Munk's seen. He works nights and drinks days now, but he's done every kind of job in every place. Handles the machinery at Setton's now, because he likes to set himself apart by running his routine at odds. Likes to be pissed at ten thirty in the morning and if anyone can really tell me a good reason why not to then I'd go with it and judge him, but until that time... He's seen it all, a lot of things, the world, and he knows what he's choosing and he knows what the alternatives were.

It's like watching a blind man skating to see Munk talk, he only needs one real word a sentence and you're hanging on it; can't believe he's going to get from a to b. This one day I'm eating a fish finger sandwich on the wall by our place, and it's quite sunny and I see him come by, a practised drunk like, who knows how to walk in a straight line. He stops by the wall and starts rolling a fag, looking pretty tanned considering. He has these washed out green eyes and he figures you out with them, though he doesn't care.

He says like, 'Fish fingers is it.'

'And brown sauce.'

'Oh aye.'

'Want half?' I go. Fish finger sandwiches was what my mother used to make me when I was ill.

Munk now, he eyes mine. He goes, 'Pfff' though. His fingers work round the fag paper like I don't think he has much feeling. 'Tell you right; I'll tell you, fish fingers, like *how much work*, for your fish fingers. No no.' One hand held up, because he expects an argument. 'Wouldn't know, you *would not know*. Used to work, boat like, out by Denmark, fish fingers. Brrr. And this weather. You wouldn't know, storms. Water. Up here.' He raises his hand to show me how the water must have made the horizon. Never looks at you when he's talking – or at anything else that's around him. He looks straight through thin air to whatever he wants to see. 'Weather. Terrible. Rain, oh, water.' Past his swimming arms the waves are like sea monsters. He's making the sounds of the ocean. You can't watch Munk tell a story without smiling. 'Waves, crsshhh, crssshhhh! Rain. Brrrr,' and his fingers pick droplets that fly at his face. 'Ping! ping! ping! Hard. So no. You go on, eat your fish fingers. Now you know like. Brrrrrr.'

I'd like to do justice to a man like Munk and explain what makes him special – that he's not just a drunk in some shit little town. It's men like Munk that hold the wisdom of the world and that's why they stop trying to keep up with it.

I asked Munk if he knows that guy with the ponytail. Part of me hasn't stopped thinking about that day. Part of me wanted to say Hey, Mr Woodwork Teacher, stop worrying. Pick yourself up. Because we've all got our shit to deal with; no one needs to spread it round. Come out to the Lion on a Saturday. Everyone here has to get by.

Katie's really beautiful to me. Not as beautiful as when she was a little girl, and she knows this; she never lets herself forget this, but she's very beautiful to me. I like her when she's just woken up and her face gets soft and undefended. I like the shape of her lips. I like how she knows what I'm thinking. And how I never know, vice versa. What's in her mind. It could be anything.

We had a row a couple of nights ago. She says to me, 'You're not going to be a removals man for the rest of your life.'

And I say I don't know. Nobody knows what's around the next corner.

I went down the river after actually, the flat's too small for screaming. She gets premenstrual; she starts saying nothing's good enough, but I was remembering us walking home together that night. Summertime, so it had still been twilight. We crossed the bridge and stood looking over the handrail. We spotted objects in the water. I saw a wheel; she saw a skull. Maybe a dog's or a fox's. We stood there with the black middle of the water running out around us, imagining how they might have fallen in.

All the boys in town jump off the bridge, one point or another. You don't want to get to High School and still be a virgin on it. I coached my brother one week a couple of years ago, a hot summer when his time was coming up. Just close your eyes, I told him, like it's only three foot down.

It was dark by the time I got there, the day before yesterday. It's almost November now. On the other side of the river the houses all have balconies leaning over, where the water's fall is at its highest. You'd think the noise of it would keep those people up at night. Not that I ever moved anyone in or out of there. I never heard how loud it is inside.

I must have sat on the bench a good few hours. I didn't take my phone so I'm not sure. I saw a bird. I thought they were all asleep by the time it's dark but it was sitting up on the walls by those leaning houses, moving around underneath the streetlight that lights the bridge. It spotted me, one eye stare. It was black.

This bird, it doesn't know the answer to two plus two. It doesn't have a clue that its genes are made out of DNA. It doesn't know how to plug a wire into a socket and find out any piece of information in the world, but I swear this bird looks at me like not all of us can have wings.

Something that occurs to me is that often it's other people's opinions that make us think that we need more. It's what we reckon we ought to have, the great unknown. How everyone else might judge us. Katie worries that she's a failure but who sets that measurement? A failure in comparison to what? Munk wins eighty quid on a scratch card then sticks half of it into the one arm bandit. That's failure. I mean, it's not failure to be happy. She screams sometimes. Totally beats herself up and I try to tell her, failure doesn't mean anything. It's just a random word that we came up with a meaning for.

She goes, 'I'm trapped here and I'm never going to get anywhere else.' And I try to put my arms around her but it's times like that she hates me.

This one time, she got drunk on cider on her own at home. When I got back she had this burn on her back, midway up, which she'd got against the heater. Maybe she hadn't known it was happening, or she'd done it on purpose. She looked like she thought it was clever, one in the eye for me. As if I wanted to make her trapped. If people want to leave they just get up and go.

If she did go – and this is the truth – came back for a holiday and found me and Munk down the Lion probably; if she walked in with that look you get from moving house, in a lot of ways I'd be glad for her. I'd like to see her do well. I really would. Her potential's like this extra inch of clothes around her now.

We haven't made up yet. The flat's full of all this quiet that isn't quiet at all. I've spent a lot of time the last few days just out and about. I was on East Street again in fact – yesterday. Just as empty as half-day closing now it's the end of the year. I didn't see that guy there though. In one of the windows or walking out of a door, or inching along down the street asking *Why?* for a second time.

But this is the thing I wanted to tell you. I did give it a go. I don't know if anybody saw me. I put down my beer on the wall where I was sitting. I went ahead and did it like him. I asked the sky my question. If someone saw me, whatever. Whatever anyway.

But this is what happened. It was the craziest thing. Out from behind me, there must have been two hundred birds, more, three or four hundred, I don't know. The very second I raised my hands. Flying synchronised, the way they do in the autumn time. All of them in the street, from tree to tree. Taking over the road, every one of them joined up by nothing, but all of them knowing exactly how to fly.

So many of them together, so silent. I couldn't even hear one wing. It was the most beautiful, wonderful thing.

I wanted to tell him. I don't know if he lives on East Street. Maybe it's pointless hanging out there. Yesterday I couldn't leave. I sorted through the ways I could paint the picture for him. I didn't like to think he might come out when I wasn't there.

I didn't like to think of him opening his door onto an empty street – when I haven't forgotten him – and there might be something he still needs that I could share.

Recreation

One night, Christine lost her fear and woke Doug up in the darkness. It was four thirteen a.m. – the quiet, red eyes of God stared out from her alarm clock – nothing else in the room was visible.

'Dougie...' she said, 'Dougie, I have to talk to you.'

First he made a sound. He attempted to rouse himself.

'Dougie...'

He breathed, 'It's the middle of the night.'

'I've been awake.'

Now, with his movement, she felt the solidity of the space, could feel the presence of the furnishings she knew. For the past hour, small sounds in one or other quarter of the room, or the rest of the house, had orientated her.

He rolled over and placed one of his arms across her in order to appease her without speaking, but she couldn't let him sleep. Underneath the covers, she took hold of his hand. She felt its soft hairs and the tiny, dry ridges of his palm.

'Tell me a fantasy,' she said.

Finally he answered, 'What fantasy?'

'A fantasy. A sexy story. Some fantasy you have.'

She negotiated his silence.

Her fingers climbed between his. She began herself, 'I've been having fantasies. I've been fantasising. I'll tell you mine.'

'I've got to be up in three hours.'

'I know.'

She lay quietly, gathering courage until she no longer felt that there was enough space for her silence.

'I imagine... that we're in a room full of people. Some of them are friends; some of them are strangers. Sometimes we film it. We're there to lose all our inhibitions. We don't care about... the rules; it's not a dirty thing – we just care about pleasure. We all take off each other's clothes. We just care about being free. I watch them take yours off; you're wearing your blue suit. Two women undo your tie, and your shirt; they start running their hands over your chest; they touch your nipples. A man is kneeling in front of you and he unzips your fly...'

Somewhere in the loose dark beside her, she heard her husband draw a breath. It could have been excitement – or frustration with her – or a kind of distaste, she didn't know.

She continued to tell him. 'He reaches into your trousers. And you're so hard, because there's three different people's hands touching you and... if you closed your eyes, you wouldn't know who was who.

People bring me over to you, so I can watch the man who's kneeling put you in his mouth.'

Doug's breath came again but still she couldn't tell the difference – if he was now aroused or if disgust was the content of the sound. It wasn't that she wanted to hurt him.

'Now the two women beside you, they undress themselves. I start touching one, her breasts. I rub my hands... I rub my palms... all over them. And the other, she bends down and she puts her nipple in your mouth. You start licking it, but you're helpless because this man is– '

'Christine,' he said quietly, 'stop.'

She lay still, the darkness infecting her. 'Why?' she asked. But he didn't answer, so she went on. 'You're helpless because... you can't do anything except just take what he's doing to you. He's got these strong hands, holding you, and he opens his own fly. And the woman is kissing me.'

His silence was a part of the bed. It was a piece of the room.

'Why stop?' she asked him.

'It's not wrong,' she said.

'I want more.' She tried to explain, 'It's not just sex.' It was everything. She didn't believe in freedom anymore. She no longer hoped for the things she'd once wanted her life to be. She was afraid of the real world.

The next day, neither Doug nor Christine mentioned the occurrences of the night. Work began and ended at the same times as usual but when Christine returned to the house, he wasn't there. Usually he arrived at least half an hour before her; she worked in Ealing. Christine read a novel for twenty minutes, drank wine, planned dinner, and eventually she called Doug's mobile phone but he had switched it off.

She'd never been aware of needing fantasies. They had crept into her life. They'd come to hover in corners, to sit in the kitchen when she made lunch. In truth, she didn't want them. She had never been a highly sexed person; she'd always been satisfied.

It had begun in the car. She and Doug had been driving home after going to see his mother at the Cedars. She'd been almost asleep, her face against the cool window, the traffic a reverberation in her thoughts – and an image had come into her mind. The image was of a girl with very curly blonde hair, a great head of it, and before the thought had been banished, this girl had been giving Doug oral sex. Sitting up in the passenger seat, she had glanced at her husband before setting her own eyes on the road.

It was true that they didn't have a very active sex life anymore. There were things that made it impossible sometimes, even when you didn't have children. For instance, they would go to dinner with friends on Monday and he might work late on Tuesday night; perhaps on Wednesday she would get caught up in *Newsnight* and by the time she looked he'd be asleep. Thursday night he always went for drinks. And during the weekends, in those moments when sex might happen, quietness would sometimes fall instead, to make fifteen years a barrier between them – as if none of those years had in fact been shared.

It had occurred to her that they might be experiencing the beginning of the end as far as their sex life was concerned, but she hadn't anticipated this little maelstrom of fantasies.

Doug didn't get home until one a.m. and by that time she was drunk. He came to stand in the living room and look in silence at the television while she stared up at him, at his expression – unsettled, unresolved. She waited for an explanation but none came.

'You enjoy yourself last night then, did you?' he said finally. And, before she could answer him, he left the room.

'Doug...?' she said, 'Doug?' following him upstairs to the bathroom. She pushed open the edge of the door, allowing all yellow light to spill, showing him before the mirror.

'I have feelings too,' he told her, his toothbrush in one hand.

The next day they had plans. It was several months since they had arranged their trip to Cornwall to see the Eden Project. There are over a million different plants inside its great motionless arks, she'd read.

She is very concerned with ecological issues – recycling has been made far easier now anyway. But generally she has become more liberal with the years, in opposition to what is described as the majority flow, where age brings greater financial security, which in turn brings conservatism. Sometimes she and Doug looked through environmentalist websites in the evening. They had not only broadband but Wi-Fi now.

When morning arrived though, Doug got out of bed with the alarm and dressed in his office clothes. Eight weeks' notice was required of him for any annual leave.

She pretended to be asleep for a while, scared to speak, but it became obvious that he would exit the room in silence.

'I don't want to go on my own,' she said.

He didn't seem to know how to look at her. 'I'd rather work now.'

They'd both planned to keep their phones off for three days. Christine had been imagining it; anticipating wandering under the great growths of foreign trees, through microclimates. It had been a little like a science fiction film in her mind, or *Charlie and the Chocolate Factory*. They have always been garden-lovers, park-goers.

Doug picked up his coat, his briefcase; he shrugged and did not look happy as he left the room.

Christine called him at eleven o'clock, just to see if he had changed his mind, but in the end the Eden Project went unvisited.

They were planning to travel the world once retired. It was their shared intention to visit all seven of the Natural Wonders, for which the votes would be counted by then. It was likely that Jeju Island in South Korea would feature. She wanted to stand up on its scalloped, neon green plateau and feel herself become one of the tiny people captured in the many aerial photographs. The consensus was that Table Mountain in South Africa would make the list as well, where more species were contained than now existed in Europe.

For several periods of hours over the next few days, not at work, she sat googling locations from the shortlist. They had already been saving for over seven years. They have always been prudent with money and childlessness gifts a disposable income – as it should more recreation time, though in reality that was often consumed by their jobs.

She pictured the deck of a cruise liner; both of them with entirely white hair. Should she have attempted to conceive, she wonders now. Only medication, hormone pills, would have raised her chances from twenty to eighty percent. In some way, the idea of kids had only ever left her feeling scared. But if they had had them, the weekends might now be filled with comings and goings – for instance, they might have a Sunday lunch, galleries and things which might not be possible with kids.

It isn't unusual not to want children now though. The world is full already.

On Saturday, Christine went shopping alone and spent four hundred pounds in *Agent Provocateur*. She stood in front of the mirror with a candelabra on either side and saw her nipples in a peephole bra. She brought the things home and laid them out on the bed in their little nests of tissue paper. When Doug came back from The Gunners and saw them there though, he only picked them up one by one and placed them in a pile on the ottoman. He sat down on the bed's edge, slowly took off his shoes and did not look around at her as she began to cry.

Why do we bother wanting things we can't have? When we are adults and can see the difference clearly, it doesn't make us happy to churn out these fantasies. It doesn't change our lives.

On Sunday afternoon, Christine prepared herself to confront him and resolve the rift. She chose a bottle of Australian Cabernet to oil the wheels. She stood in Tesco's, in front of the selection, considering what the price might be for an Ayers Rock or outback tour. It was five minutes to four and the supermarket was near to closing, harbouring only the sounds of the ventilation system and of restock boxes being dragged across tiled floors.

In this calm before the storm, her imagination nurtured pictures: tropical waters and the fauna of coral reefs. On the one and only scan she'd undergone, for diagnosis, the ineffective follicles within her ovaries had uncoiled like coral leaves.

He was watching television in the living room when she returned. She carried the bottle into the kitchen. She brought two glasses, each two-thirds full, and placed them on the coffee table in front of him.

He was willing to meet her eyes, but not for very long, and not in order to communicate more than a kind of stubbornness. As if he was determined to hold onto the feelings she'd given him, despite the fact that they were feelings of inadequacy.

On the television, an attractive, active looking young woman was explaining what it meant to work in the field of paleotempestology. Christine took the remote control from his hand. They remained in this still life, the television muted, as she weighed up what to say.

'I'm sorry. I'm sorry if I've been making you feel unhappy. That's not what I wanted to do.'

'What did you want?' he asked her. 'What did you expect?'

'I didn't have any expectations.'

'You're not happy with us,' he said, turning to see the TV screen as though its silent images could give him an answer he preferred. Sepia-toned photographs of storms were progressing there. He finished, 'Completely out of the blue.'

'I had to get my courage up.'

'Is that what you want? You want to start doing that kind of thing?'

'I don't know. I'm scared.' She wanted to explain to him but did not know how. 'I feel like there's nothing left to explore.'

'That's a very cruel thing to say. I'm sorry if all I've got to offer is me. Do you want to have sex with other people?'

'Doug,' she said, 'I don't want to *live* in a fantasy...' She wanted to tell him though, how she felt possibilities narrowing, chances winking out. She wanted to tell him how the normal world had made an acquisition of her life. But she couldn't. He didn't want her to say those things.

For a number of minutes they spoke no words to each other, at first occupying each other's silences, but after a time – seeing the images on the TV screen – watching

in mutual absorption reruns of hurricanes destroying
streets and tsunamis sweeping parklands away.

We Wanted To Give You Something

It was a Tuesday in April when she came home and told her parents that they had found a place to live. She parked in what she realised was no longer her street, in the bare lee of spring. Her mother had started saying that they'd hear the first cuckoo soon. By the 24th – she said it every April. Where this date came from had never quite been explained; a little dividend of pocket wisdom, brought out again on each of the like-for-like years.

At the estate agents they'd signed the contracts and then she had dropped him home; he didn't drive. They touched hands eagerly and awkwardly when she wasn't changing gear. Winter had left them under a new vociferous blue sky.

His family was only his mother – he had a father and they did speak, but he referred to him as Peter. Peter lived on the other side of town with Christine.

The cul de sac was as uninhabited as always. His

mother moved the net curtain and relinquished it as he climbed out, lifting his bag from the footwell. And holding the car door open with his body, he offered her a wind-scattered smile. 'Here we go then.'

Words that she reciprocated.

She drove home, in moments feeling like someone new.

Her mother called out from the kitchen as she took her key from the door, asking how it had gone.

'It went well. Really well,' she replied, causing her mother to walk through to the hall.

They told her father and together discussed the details. She talked about various things in her room, familiar possessions and how they'd look in the new flat. She tried to use words that included them; when you come and have dinner, she said, when you want to sleep in the spare room.

She took them round to see it on Thursday: number fourteen, Iris House. The corridor outside was narrow but carpeted, without windows.

'No natural light,' her mother said, walking abreast, holding her bag in both her hands.

Unlocking, there wasn't enough room for them to enter together. Her father hung back, examining the other numbered doors.

Once they were inside though, they said only good things. She'd already brought a few boxes, some of her own and some of his. Her mother opened the cupboards, looked at the window fastenings and moved the table on its legs. Her father put his hands in his pockets. He was too tall to get through the doors properly, so he entered and left the rooms without moving further than their thresholds. He suggested making an inventory noting any small areas of damage.

He and her mother stood in front of the balcony without opening the French windows and admired the view. It was why she'd chosen the place she told them. As soon as she'd seen it, she'd known it was the right home. She talked about how it would look at night and in the mornings, but all she really wanted to say to them was *I love you*. She watched them examining different distant places through the glass and there was nothing else that she had any desire to say.

During the evenings that week, they transported the rest of his boxes. He carried them down the path and they packed them into the car together. His mother stood on the doorstep and asked if she was happy driving with so full a car.

The boxes made a playground in the empty living room and kitchen, in the bedroom on top of the unclothed bed. It was a little sad and strange at home now, she told him. Her father had started fixing things of hers that were broken.

'They can come round all the time,' he said. 'I like them. It's not far away.' She agreed but he could see this changed nothing. He told her, 'I love you'. He looked into her face and really told her, like he was trying to say something else, like he was trying to assure her that the love he had for her meant this transition would be worthwhile.

It rained on the moving in day, Easter Sunday, and the wind was very hard. They helped to carry her final things, which were bags now, her washbag and suitcase, down the road to the car. Each of the nearby parking spaces had been taken.

Afterwards, they sat in the family kitchen back home eating Marmite and tomato sandwiches, the sounds of the heating and the wind alternating, the grey shapes of the cherry tree's branches in motion outside. Her mother opened a bottle of wine and she had a quarter of a glass.

She felt she needed to mark the moment but didn't know how. Her mother carefully poured the tiny wine.

'Did you get your shampoo from by the bath?' her father said. 'I don't know if you wanted to take it.' He stood with his back to the sink and held his glass. Every time they ushered out another detail she was closer to having to go.

They hadn't bought any Easter eggs, what with all the activity. She said, 'Remember when we had that Easter egg hunt and all the eggs had little notes round them.'

'If you want to find the treasure, look to the place where you're at leisure…'

'Under my pillow.'

'Well we always tried hard with that sort of thing,' he said.

Across the table, her mother sat with her feet up on a chair, her shoes kicked off to one side. They traded a look, upon which her father was induced to straighten and open the cupboard above the kettle and the coffee and tea. With no backs, all the kitchen cupboards revealed blue wall behind the shelves. The rest of the kitchen had been painted yellow five years ago, but they hadn't taken the cupboards down to paint the wall behind.

He said, 'We wanted to give you something.' He handed it to her, wrapped in a padding of clean kitchen roll. 'Don't get excited,' he said. 'We didn't buy it. It's not a new set of car keys or anything.'

For a moment she held it without unwrapping it.

He added, 'You'll probably never use it for anything.'

'She might have exactly the right thing for it,' her mother said. 'You don't know.'

'It's from both of us.'

Inside the kitchen roll was a tiny wooden box. It was plain, but obviously old and delicately made.

'It's empty,' her father said, 'just in case you thought it had anything in it.'

'We would've liked to fold up a few fifty pound notes in there,' her mother shrugged and laughed.

It was about as long as her thumb. The lid swivelled neatly open.

'It's from just after when we moved in together,' her mother said.

'I found it in a second hand shop then.'

The wood was warm in the midst of the warm paper – underneath the cupboards, there were strip-lights to light the counters which heated up the bases of the cupboards and anything that was put inside.

She swivelled its lid open and closed again and thanked them.

He said, 'We wanted to put something in it. I said some potpourri or something.'

'We thought you'd probably find something you wanted to keep in it. You can use it for anything.' There was momentary silence. 'He's a lovely guy,' her mother said. 'We're glad you found such a lovely guy.' After a few moments she called to her husband with a tilt of her head, winding her arm around him as he approached.

'He's great,' her father said.

She looked at them both. 'I love you,' she told them.

They watched her rewrap the box. She thought about staying one more night. She couldn't do that though. Her boyfriend would be waiting with his own last boxes. He would be watching for sets of headlights on the street outside.

The parents stayed together in the kitchen after she'd left. They finished the wine. He watched her sit up and pull her shoes towards her with the point of one bare foot. For the last two weeks her toenails had been red.

'It's lasted well, that box,' he said. 'I mean, not that it got used.' And then he said, 'Was it the shop they had by the launderette?'

'I can't remember. They had lovely things there. I don't know if they went bust or they just retired; I don't think they went bust. They were getting by in the end.'

He remembered and agreed. There was the sound of continuing rain outside. He said, 'God, it's funny isn't it.' He took the empty wine bottle from the table.

She looked up at him. She stood and put her arms around his waist, under his own, and felt the wine bottle settle against her back.

'You're so warm,' she told him. He always was. From

just above her head, she heard him answering that he loved her.

In this new place, the overhead lights were bright on the bare cream carpet and the walls. Their boxes were piled on top of each other and they had to squeeze between. She listened to him unwrapping their own bottle of wine as she went between the little rooms. Our bedroom, she thought, our bathroom. The living room sounded best; she presented him with the words as she returned.

It was too cold for them to sit outside. Their balcony possessed a pair of chairs that seemed to be staring at the view themselves. She listened to see if she could hear what the neighbours were doing. There was an undercurrent of sound that might have been a toilet cistern or shower.

'It's a pretty good place for a first home,' he said, handing her one glass.

She grinned. 'For sure.' He could boast about a cheese sandwich.

'Have you seen on the shelves?' He showed her the dust-free, irregular shadows left behind by the previous tenant's books. There were also empty picture hooks on the walls.

She talked about how it was exciting to think of who might have lived here before. She liked the idea of one couple growing on, going further, and of another coming to inhabit their place. 'You think it was a couple that lived here?' she said.

He told her he didn't care. He reached out and put a hand on her thigh, watching her face.

They drank the bottle quickly; he filled the glasses before they were empty. They sat with their backs against the walls or the flat's navy blue settee, not bothering to move unopened boxes off its seats. At one point they lay on their backs on the floor. They talked about how long they would probably stay here. A year, maybe even two, maybe more. Later, when she was nearly drunk, she took out the tiny wooden box and showed it to him. She talked about her parents and for a little while she cried.

'It's a lovely present,' he said. 'They love you a lot.' And then he took the cork from the almost empty bottle of wine. 'You're only meant to do this with champagne corks,' he told her. He took out a handful of change and she watched him sort carefully through it. She felt a deep affection for the way he held his change. 'You make a slit in the cork and then you put the fifty pence in. It's for good luck.' He glanced up. 'It's tradition.'

She watched him make it, moving his hands with his head bent over.

'Why do you love me?' she said.

'I don't know.' He stopped, but he didn't want to stop. He went on again with the cork and the coin. 'Because of the things you say to me?' He wanted it to be the right answer. He said, 'Because of how you make me feel.'

'Anyone who loved you would say those things.'

He retrieved the box from the carpet and put the cork inside it. He gave it back to her, shut once more, observing her as she reopened it.

'Because you chose me,' he tried again.

Lisa

Lisa came on one of these work placements for people who are long-term unemployed and, without being cruel, it really wasn't hard to see why. Lisa was fat, which isn't enough in itself of course; plenty of fat people in this world have jobs. But she had an attitude. At first I only picked up on it a little, an offhandedness. The kind of manner that just doesn't get you by in life. Arrogant, though she was shy as well, and her shyness was sweet. When she smiled her whole face did light up.

She'd speak in these little blusters or cut you off or end up not even looking at you. She had skills – typing; she could use Excel. That's what she ended up doing for us mostly, the database stuff none of us had time for. I remember how she answered the phone when she first started, because that was meant to be one of her duties. That was one of the areas that Simon thought we'd be able to help her up-skill.

The phone would ring. She'd pick it up. She'd go, 'Yeh?'

Apparently she used to answer the phone for her dad's business too.

Anyway, she started off just doing Tuesdays. Tuesdays was the day she was meant to do, because one day a week was about as much of a workload as we had to give her. She was slow but there's a limit to the number of databases any business needs. But the thing was, it made her happy to come into the office. It started almost immediately. 'Oh if you need that I could come in on Thursday' or 'Oh you'll probably want me a couple of days next week to sort all that out.' Ever so pleased with herself, making a big favour out of it. But then, if you told her that she'd done something well, as I say, she could be very sweet. Light up like that. 'What will you do when I'm gone?' she started saying.

So she fitted in perfectly well. No one had any issue with her. I can't really think that she would have had an issue with anyone. There's a lot of people who can't even get voluntary work placements these days. I'm sure she must have been glad.

But let me give you an example of one of the things that acted as a little warning sign for me. She had this car and, I'm not exaggerating, the door was taped on. It was the passenger door luckily because Lisa would have had some trouble climbing over the gear stick to get in and out. You should have seen sometimes what she'd eat for lunch. As a matter of fact my car was also in an awful state. I'd been badly hit in it not long before and I'd needed to have it panel beaten back into shape. I have a new one now.

So I joked to her that she was the only person in the world with a car worse than mine.

'I've got a Range Rover actually,' she said.

A black one, brand new, which she'd only ever driven once. This is what she told me. Her boyfriend borrowed it.

She'd never mentioned a boyfriend before, but she started telling me now. It began with his job, which was an exceptionally good job. Then where he lived, which was more than two hundred miles away.

'Oh,' I said. 'What a shame.' Because long distance relationships can be quite difficult.

Then she told me that they would be moving in together soon. At that time she lived with her parents and she hated it. Well she wasn't alone there. I told her that.

'Great,' I said. 'That's wonderful.'

There was an article in *The National Enquirer* recently called World's Fattest Bride. Some people are actually excited by fat. In this article, the woman, Susanna, had got to fifty seven stone and wanted to be heavier for the wedding. Her husband-to-be was a chef. He'd wheel Susanna to the table. He liked to feed her out of his hand. So in fact you can never tell.

Lisa did well. The placement was doing her a lot of good. At first she'd hardly talked at all but after a few weeks she was communicating properly, having lunch at the same time as everyone and whatnot. There weren't any difficulties for her.

It's not a big company, our company. I work in marketing there. That sounds pretty high flying, but to be honest it's just a lot of poster and flyer printing and distributing; we have a newsletter that goes out by email, I update the website, things like that. I do gather a lot of statistics. We analyse who's buying and who's not and who's buying less or more than they were buying previously. We sell pet accessories. There's a level to which pet accessories are recession-proof, but after that they're not.

I don't have a pet myself. Lisa said she had a dog but I never saw her with any dog hairs on her, or even on the seats of that car. She never for instance once showed any interest in anything from the dog range we produce.

Three months passed, which was the limit of her voluntary work placement. They don't make them carry on for that long. But then at the end of it, Lisa decided that she wanted to stay.

By this point it was probably true that to an extent Simon did rely on her. Wednesdays we had our team meetings. She'd started coming for them. She answered the phone better, 'Hello, Man's Best Friend,' though she even managed to say that defensively. Lisa was constantly on the verge of being defensive. She was a naturally defensive person. I don't know when she became fat but I bet she was defensive first.

Her birthday came and at our company we like to make a point of celebrating everyone's birthdays, so Simon asked her what sort of flowers she liked, which is a pretty difficult question to answer defensively.

'I don't actually like flowers,' she goes to him. 'Don't bother getting me any flowers. It doesn't matter what kind they are; I won't like them.'

What kind of person doesn't like flowers? Or talks that way to her boss. No wonder she was in voluntary employment. Myself, I've never taken benefits of any kind.

Of course, the thing was, because it was voluntary, actually he wasn't her boss. Actually it did mean that she was doing him a favour. And that was what she started getting more and more inflated by. She didn't need to be polite, not to any of us really and not to Simon. The offhandedness just grew.

The fact of the matter was, she didn't want to get back into proper employment. Didn't care a fig about any reference she might get from Simon. Perhaps she even believed he was going to offer to pay her eventually. Well the company didn't have that kind of money.

I want to share something with you. I'm not someone who criticises benefit scroungers. I keep my opinions to myself. But this is what Lisa told me, of her own volition.

'How's it going getting your flat with your boyfriend then?' I asked her.

'We're getting it now,' she said. When she smiled, she actually blushed. She went half-red.

'Lovely,' I said. 'That's wonderful.' I asked her to tell me more about it. She started telling me this and that.

Then she said, 'My friends don't want us to move in together though. They'd be happier if we broke up. They don't like him because he's got a job and none of them have ever had jobs. They hate anyone who's got a job.'

This is no word of a lie.

'But I'm not like that,' she said.

She said this boyfriend of hers was a lawyer – earning sixty pounds an hour. These men who are attracted to morbidly obese women though, presumably they come in all walks of life.

Anyway, I said something to her like, 'Wow. Sixty pounds an hour. So he bought you the Range Rover I suppose.'

No she says. He didn't buy her the Range Rover. And she started telling this story about how she worked somewhere where she made this massive amount of money. There weren't a lot of details. She'd speak like that, in flurries, little scatterguns, so I can't remember just exactly why or how it was that she was supposed to have come by this Range Rover, which she said she'd bought new and driven once before letting her rich lawyer boyfriend drive it instead.

I didn't say anything to anyone of course, but I did begin to think.

It was about the fourth or fifth month she was with us when Lisa came in with her news. I was making tea for everyone and I asked her if she also wanted tea.

'Yes please,' she said. You could already see that something was different. She could hardly contain herself.

'You look very happy,' I said. And I asked her did she want one sugar or two that day, because she'd been struggling with the process of cutting down.

'I'm on a new diet,' she said. 'I have to lose weight. The doctor's told me. Because I'm going to have a baby.'

For a good half an hour, no one got any work done. We had the tea and we talked about scans and we talked about names and how she and her boyfriend were going to be getting their place together soon. Simon came out and sat with us and he has three children of his own so he had plenty to share.

She sat there on her chair in the middle of us all. She seemed absolutely transported of course.

'Are you going to get married then?' I asked her.

'Actually we don't believe in marriage,' she said. 'We think having a baby's enough of a bond, even more than getting married could ever be.'

I never asked her what her boyfriend's name was. Or if I asked her I've forgotten what she said. *My boyfriend* was the only way she ever referred to him. That was something that came to me later on.

Now Lisa was pregnant of course, she couldn't lift anything, though sometimes I needed help with boxes of stock. Her back started aching too – though how it had survived up until that point, who knew.

She spent a tremendous time talking to Simon especially. Simon's two boys were six and four and his daughter was about eighteen months old. When Simon's wife had had the little girl, Jessica, she brought her into the office to show everyone. We said to Lisa she'd have to do the same.

She stuck to her diet. No sugar in her tea, only eating Maltesers for treats, and I suppose you could say her lunches did improve. I was curious then to see how much it was possible for someone of her size to 'show' though.

Anyway she moved into her flat; her boyfriend was still working in Cardiff. Obviously he couldn't give up such a good job. 'How are these friends of yours taking to him?' I asked her.

But for a while everything was fine. And then, don't get me wrong, but just about the time when talking about her pregnancy started wearing thin for us, that was exactly the time that it started to sound like things weren't quite so fine for Lisa any more.

Her boyfriend had said this and that; they'd had a row about this and that. Her boyfriend had been asked away on a stag weekend to coincide with her due date. What did we think about that? Well now we all had to gee Lisa up. She'd be fine, we said. But not only that, her mother and sister were going away on the date that the baby was due as well. She was going to be completely on her own. What did we think about that? Well, we'd be there for her we said. Mobile phone numbers started getting handed out.

So the due date came – Lisa kept on working with us right up until the week beforehand. She was fine, she said. She'd rather be working, she said. Apart from her backache she wasn't uncomfortable. And right up to the end, I swear you couldn't see a bump, just that same shocking stomach.

It was Simon who got the call – or the text, in fact. Lisa sent him a picture of the baby.

Two weeks later was the day she arranged to bring the baby in. And in she came, but she didn't bring him with her. Josh, she'd called him. Josh was with her parents. She showed us another photograph of him.

At half past ten that same night though, Simon got the message. The baby was sick – it was in intensive care. And then a message two hours later, saying she was at the hospital. The last message came, he said when he'd gathered us around in the office the next day, at half past two in the morning, telling him Josh had died.

It's no exaggeration; it's no word of a lie when I say Lisa was back in the office two days later. We all said to her she didn't need to come.

'I feel better if I'm here,' she told us. 'It gives me something to do. I don't have to think about Josh.'

We all nodded. We said we understood. But you could have cut that air with a knife.

She sat back in her chair. We had tea. Simon got biscuits. We hugged her. No one answered the phone. She was red faced but she wasn't red eyed. She was red faced and taking two sugars again but I'm telling you, she didn't look a bit different than she had the first day she'd walked into our office. That baby had come and gone without a trace.

'Are you sure you want to be in?' Lindy asked her.

But she said she couldn't bear to be at home. She said that her boyfriend was still away.

I don't know anything about childbirth. Personally I don't want to have any children. Not every woman has to have a child. People say, you can get a dog. But I don't need to own a pet either. I have no gap to fill.

I don't know anything about pregnancy or motherhood, but I know something about human nature. I know enough about human nature to feel – *intuit* – when something isn't right.

Simon touches my arm halfway through the day. Again Lisa's having tea. No one can get on with the work they're meant to do. How can we get on with our work when she's sitting in the middle of the room three days after losing her child?

He touches my arm. He makes a little sign that we should go into his office.

'Vera,' he says, once the door is closed. 'Vera, I have a question to ask you, and I want you to be completely honest with me. What do you think of Lisa?' he says.

So I say to him, 'I like her.' But I can see he's waiting for more. I can see suddenly that there's something on his own lips. Well I'm an honest person. I don't need to hide anything from anyone. 'I'm not sure she really owns a Range Rover...' I tell him.

And he nods over this slowly. 'And are there any other things you don't believe?' he says then. 'Is there anything else she's told you?'

I look at him very closely. I see how troubled he is – the size of the thing he doesn't want to say out loud to me. So I tell him, yes. Sometimes I do get the feeling that she's not being honest. But I don't want to say she never grew an inch. That she looks just the same as she always did. That no one should be in work three days after losing their first child.

We haven't ever spoken a word between us – Lindy and Simon, Anagrette, myself – not a word of disbelief between us.

'I've had some doubts,' Simon starts telling me now though, 'and I'm not the only one, it seems. Lindy's been having some doubts. And Lindy's husband's a doctor.

I've noticed on Facebook as well,' he says, 'I haven't seen any status updates from Lisa that have anything to do with the baby.'

Well I'm not on Facebook but she's mentioned *exactly this* to me and I tell him now: she isn't speaking about it online. I tell him how she explained to me that she thinks it cheapens it, to post your pregnancy news on a website. How she said she wasn't going to put up any pictures – wasn't even going to announce the birth. I didn't think twice about it I say. I don't use websites like that. I didn't think about it when it should have made alarm bells clang.

But why would she lie to us? I ask him. What would make her do that? For attention? Or to laugh about us when she's not here?

Simon's putting all these pieces together himself still though, and I can see him failing to know what he should do. He has some kind of responsibility towards Lisa of course. He may not be employing her but she's come to trust to him. A bond of trust has formed between us all.

For instance the way she's sitting as Simon and I walk back out into the office. Nobody's working still. It's hard to believe – all this time, all of us feeling that something was wrong, intuiting it, but no one ever voicing a single word.

She sits on the chair that's hers now, talking about the memorial to Lindy, Lindy nodding with a face full of concern and sympathy. But in fact Lindy doesn't believe her. And in the corner, Anagrette, one hand covering her mouth – nothing but compassion. I get to my own chair, but I don't sit down. I look into my colleagues' eyes. And I look at Lisa.

'What's the meaning of this?' I say. I feel the lie. She's sitting there, just drinking her tea. She looks up as though she doesn't understand. As though she's the victim of course. And I feel Simon touch my arm again, but I don't care. 'What's the meaning of this? Well Lisa? Tell me the truth! Well Lisa? *Lisa!*' I say.

The Fairytale Of Esmerelda

Here we come to it. In the very middle of the dark, at the night's hub, here stands the Circus. Black ground stoops its way to this, the shadows and the runnels and the cracks wend their way to this, in the wind's arms the Circus is come, its face of lights raised to a starless sky.

Enter. The admission gates are arched, golden. The great queue is eaten, each last step. Wondering whisptail voices are all the wind gets, half-tickets; needless halves. Come inside, between taut canvas and silk, the stretching stripes that cover the central dome. The dome and all its vaulted air, its thousand seats, and its Ring, where breath is trapped.

Esmerelda is the Circus's child; its illustrious name. She is its desire. And this moment is the moment before she emerges. The Ring is set, the audience eye-dark, encompassing. They will see her in the flesh, once, before they wander back out to find the world made of wishes and dead ends after her.

Esmerelda will never wander anywhere.

The circumference: five elephants, proud and grey as thunderheads down, the spark of jewels needling from gold torques and cuffs. Foot-laden beasts, black eyeball gazes. There is stillness for Esmerelda.

Clowns have tumbled their way to silence at the Ring's edge – frozen, joke mouths gaping, straining upwards. Lights are trained, up, up, on the drifting ozone smoke at the dome's peak. And in their swing thread seats, the Trapeze Sisters flutter, ruffle, fall still. (Lena and Lisette. Mouths jealous-red, eyes elsewhere. It was said by one to the other once, at night, when the sound of straw is all that breaks the dark between the makeshift alleys, they could be rid of her, a little poison, twist and writhe. Oh yes it might be done. But they're not sure, in fact, that Esmerelda can be killed. Twist and writhe and she might wake refreshed. Old bent age will never get her. She doesn't sleep down in the caravans. Not one day of age will ever finger her. Lisette has seen. And they all know. Esmerelda is the Ringmaster's glory card. He keeps her under her his wing, his coat hem.)

Here he stands as the trumpets glare out, dark in all their fanfare. Upraised, outstretched, declaring Esmerelda all his own. And *now*, and *here*, all his own to give these crowds. There's a flash of pale in the shadow dome, his stare as lustrous black as love.

She comes. One nail-tip first.

A winding smoke-white arm, that nail scarlet. The toe-tip, slow leg, low stretch thigh and half her figure is revealed. And music sounds. Painted like a girl clown, little song bird, doll, enchantress. Esmerelda's celebrated image: a scarlet circle for each cheek and all other skin white, white chinadust. Rosebud, sweet lure, open-eyed, exquisite. And tonight, as she looks down on this dim moon of an audience, though too distant to be made out, she cries tears.

Across the land and every foreign country travelled, under every differing night sky, men have tumbled into love for her. Esmerelda is the mouth's first sweet opening, the first flush of wanting that every one of them has seen in some real love and lost. Innocence is beautiful because it is short, but Esmerelda's eyes are always clean of understanding what it is that she desires.

Although tonight is different. Tonight, she looks down and knows, as no one else does, that it will be her last performance. The Ringmaster is ignorant, most of all he, whom knowledge has never escaped before. The Tattooed Man, Ilus – perhaps he feels. (He's in his cage though. While the loose strands of this public wind their way between exhibits – a town of them, a marketplace outside this dome – and pass him by, Maybe he looks up, maybe he knows. As tiny gleams, see Esmerelda's secrets in his eyes.)

There is a little diamond stud set into Esmerelda's wrist, its origin long gone.

When she met the Ringmaster, as inauguration was led into his chamber, (backroom of backways, with doors in the ceiling. It can't be found: each night she's taken after, the rooms around it aren't the same) perhaps then she knew where the diamond came from. But perhaps, she now admits, it was not yet there.

(The Siamese Triplets saw her. Rake and Barcus say she was in sackcloth while Crale will insist she was bare – he's contrary and stupid; they'll ignore him, two's always company and three's a crowd – but they remember her. Pallid. Dreams in her eyes. And not beautiful. They delight in this agreement. Since Esmerelda was gathered to the bosom of the Circus, beauty is the only thing in her that's grown.)

Whether the Ringmaster found its purpose or set that jewel himself, Esmerelda's first night in his chamber became the first of many. At midnight there each time she has stood while a process is conducted. For he can take this stud from her wrist, though it's never come for her own fingers. He will place it down, will take up a small phial, and collect what Esmerelda sheds. Not blood but dove-grey dust, a little pale pour of grains: the minutes passed since midnight before. Time itself, spilling out of her.

This little gem gives Esmerelda magic. She can wing the impossible.

Yes, whether he found its purpose (what a gift! To walk into his camp without owner, urchin child, destined, ignorant of her own potential – born solely for his stage!) or whether he set it himself (and she was nothing then, just half-grown girl, normal-skinned), whichever might be the truth, that first night the Ringmaster gave Esmerelda what she dreamt of. Unparalleled and unending, five hundred years hence he told her, the light of her star would still tremble behind the hopes in every other starlet's eyes.

Esmerelda (she is told) was elated; certainly each night she feels elation when the clock turns to usher in the moment of her drum role.

Queen of weightless breath now above the crowd, she raises her arms and, with only a small launch, lifts herself into the air's fingers. Without suspension, hangs there. Extends, outlets her limbs and revolves. Slow, unreal somersault. Esmerelda can fly.

See below? You wouldn't look, your eyes entwined in her, but see him now? Dove-grey dust on his fingers. He has blown, to let a miasma of particles rise and encompass her. Between the humdrum of trapezes, Esmerelda is a pendant in a vacuum. (Lena and Lisette cling bitterly; are forced to smile.)

Each grain of sand is a moment, floating, unlocked. See the small edge of the phial in the Ringmaster's pocket? And each grain flies unbidden back to Esmerelda's skin, to be her own again.

Over the audience and its constant ovation, Esmerelda is steeped in time. Seconds are elastic to her. She dances in them.

For a long pass of uncounted evenings, performing, applauded, Esmerelda has smiled – and later been brought to his sanctum. Wrist out-held, has watched her hours trickle away from her, seen the Ringmaster stopper and store them.

Happiness she has found, and been lauded. Graced a thousand dreams, danced her floating arabesques and found no use for memory. Regretful, plaintive, pointless thing. The skill of her body has bloomed with years

217

unable to touch her. Esmerelda has lived untethered. She had been sad once, before. Now sadness cannot catch her tails.

Until tonight.

Before the hour of first curtain rise, Esmerelda has taken to seeing the circus gauntlet. (What has the Ringmaster had to fear? He's seen that she's content.) She has pretended to wander, as though she isn't seen and pointed at and whispered, but is just alike with them and no heads turn. She has meandered, dressed almost customarily, walked along the normal ground, strayed between the hawkers, punters, children, promenaders, enjoyed the tastes and smells of an earth-bound world. Like this of course, Esmerelda was finally deflowered.

As she walked the winding dissonance of the alleys, up to her tonight one bold man came. A man well-travelled, whose words were quick and sweet as, drawing her up outside the drapes of the fortune tellers' tent (where their hissed voices could be heard making high commission on easy wishes), he told Esmerelda tales of countries where no beauty like hers lived. She was a wish herself, he thought. And in his eyes, she followed rivers, crossed deserts, saw the homes of the animals she knew.

Esmerelda has her own home. White and scarlet velvet cushions; only this to show him, no other place.

And in there, for the first time, she was stranded, for it wasn't flight he wanted from her. Not weightlessness, which she knew so well and beautifully. In all the cloth and softness, he took her to the ground. Took her to touch it. Left a part of her there that she could not rescue back.

The candlelight was like safety. The drapes fell shut behind him. Heartbeats opened their hands in her chest. And though the looks she gave him were all echoes of her dancing masque, Esmerelda felt dream-dampness in the depths of her. His pause saw it; earth long-waiting under coyness and tease. And he wanted all at once, like they'd never been stirred before. He moved gentle over her.

He came to her lips, and let his tongue onto them. And open, she was touched by rivers, the filthy Ganges and the blue-sky Nile. Like deep things rising to that water's surface, a real urge came through well-learned motions. It breached her.

His slow kisses ran the circles on her cheeks. He knelt up above her to reveal the stretch of his skin – chest, navel, pubis – and Esmerelda wanted tastes. She raised her head, with glinting triumph, with something in her which was tantalising-new – all demands and buried hollows – and slight skirts slipped. An inch, another. He breathed with her, experimented with her, eyes never leaving hers. Wet fingertips in the candles' fluting shadows. Esmerelda felt him, blood-thick, felt all the stretches of miles he'd truly wandered.

Down on the floor, his hands make her body part of it. Soil rose and burrowed its arms into her. Down on the floor, she gave him her innocence to fill. Her white thighs buttocks limbs and open eating mouth. Devoured what he knew.

Later, after he had left her in her boudoir she sat and saw the look of the world through afterglow: its ranging colours and token remnants, saw the place where they'd lain – and asked herself for a simple answer. Asked herself for something that would reconcile before and after. She didn't want to lose what she had gained.

The answer that came was so immediate and complete, it seemed born of nothing, a flower of miraculous secrecy in the quiet air.

The Tattooed Man knew with his first glance. All the pictures that covered him, they stared into her, and he stared. Silent in this she stood, then gave him her question. Though she would forget, could he make a mark for her? A small depiction, to remember for her sake. She told of her single hour; short little story. She gave him the sole of one bare foot, where no one would see. A tiny image, a tiny window, ink so wonderfully crafted. A picture of a river flowing through the soil.

So Esmerelda went back to her chamber and prepared for her performance. Any doubt, loss, regret, hers till midnight only. The looking glass held a picture of her whole. Glorious colt body, which this audience now glimpses above the Ring. Limber reaches of white skin, shade-cast then, and still in the lower light of flames.

Tiny diamond winking dim.

Esmerelda drew closer to the glass, sat down on the cushioned floor and raised her sole to see her enduring answer. She let it fall, to see the rest of her. Before a reflection, explored her flesh like it was altered.

Was it altered?

Her celebrated image, though beautiful, seemed just closer to a woman's. Some quality – her charm, mystique – diminished. Less a girl child now, Esmerelda saw. In place of innocence lay something new.

And as Esmerelda turned and searched and discovered her own changes, making the most of these moments that were still hers, so it was that she came across an unexpected thing. In the soft hollow of her underarm, hidden well in alabaster skin, a tattoo of snow covered mountains. Stalled, she stared.

Esmerelda's fingers moved then, wandered the continents of her own flesh. She found a tiny ocean picture. In hidden parts, more, until her fingers fled. I for Ilus beside them. Island, forest, morning valley. So it was that Esmerelda knew.

(Occasional midnights: the Ringmaster had stood, removed the diamond from her, watched the minutes cascade. His skyless eyes had risen slowly to hers – where he'd seen no reflection left of the scarlet that had interspersed her stream, no glimmer. Evenings he has let her roam. What had he to fear?)

So Esmerelda sees. The world's landscape frightening-wide and the crescent of its populace below her. Faces upturned like dark fruits. She dances. She is choosing. Soon the music will turn into applause. And Esmerelda – amidst its clouds, crescendos – may dive a new parabola. (She isn't sure but doesn't think she'll splatter. Doubts there's liquid in her. Instead imagines becoming a thousand beads. A million grains of electric dust to water the eyes and linger above the chalk and straw of the Circus Ring. A little shimmer there, no more, a ghost to stain the air, as little care for gravity as she has ever shown.)

Esmerelda may fall. (Glissade, glissando.)

But she's not sure. She may wait. Though her phials remain, lined up with their dark-glass-gleams in multi-coloured cupboards – locked away by changeling keys secreted in the Ringmaster's coat-tails – Esmerelda may close her heart to flight. May curtsy, a final flower in the air – and later, disguise-covered, sneak. Find the golden gates. Pull upon their counterweights.

In the dark, hear only the bated breath of circus beasts, each moved to listen. Slip her gaze about the doors' gilded edge, to taste blue winter clear night. Starless. Stare out. See the wide ground there, and how it leads away.

Keeper

There is nothing unusual about the vehicle, except that its clock reads 000,005, which is unusual. She raises and casts back the garage door, revealing it without a flourish.

'Why don't you drive it?' the woman says.

The man steps between the boxes of VHS tapes and the garden wheelbarrow uninvited. He crouches down to look beneath the wheel arches. He leans in towards the passenger window, shading his eyes with nested hands.

She answers, 'I didn't want it to devalue.'

'But you've never driven it.' The woman doesn't come any nearer, either to the garage or to her. She has a blood red faux crocodile skin handbag hanging from one of her folded arms. She thinks Helen is trying to take them for the proverbial ride, but that's the last thing Helen wants.

'It's a long story,' Helen says to the woman.

The man asks for the keys.

The advert specifically states *only five miles on the clock* and this brings a fair welter of calls. Everyone is looking for a good deal – for reliability, Helen thinks. But no one likes a deal that's too good to be true. Every call she receives also harbours suspicions. As many days arrive on which new people come to view it as nights go by when the vehicle remains in the garage.

He opens the door, this man, who has come with a wide-brimmed white hat, which is easily more ostentatious than his partner's bag, and which he is now forced to remove. He is casual, but he's excited Helen sees. He surveys the unmarked interior, the upholstery, each thread of which lies in parity with the next. The vehicle has not simply been valeted.

He leans inside and deliberately displays no care in the way that he takes the front seat. He allows himself to put his hands at 'ten' and 'two'. She watches him start the engine. It starts without impediment, beginning to issue nitrogen and water vapour and carbon monoxide into the farthest quarter of the garage.

He leaves the seat. The woman looks at her own feet and at the currently empty road and the Audi they came in. At the rear of the vehicle, he presses his boot over the exhaust and releases it, over it, and releases it. His boots are Timberland and bear no relation whatsoever to the hat he is still holding. He ceases to do this and allows the exhaust smoke to once again rise around his shins.

As much as Helen dislikes the woman, without any rationale really, she is touched by a wave of fondness for the man. He is just shy of middle age and starting to run to fat, dressed smartly but in a way that speaks of effort, and he stands there attempting to pretend he doesn't want the vehicle more than he can presently remember wanting anything.

'So what's your price?' he says.

The woman with the red handbag looks on calmly from the pavement outside.

'Make me an offer,' Helen suggests to him.

'Well I don't know. What ballpark are you looking for?'

'I really couldn't say. You tell me. Make me an offer,' she responds.

She sees his gaze skim back across the bodywork.

'You must have a price in mind,' he says.

So Helen asks him, 'What do you think it's worth?'

The words always produce the same reaction – or perhaps it's the way she says them. They're not even aware they're doing it but gently, Helen sees, both of them recoil from the vehicle, its gleaming lines no longer candid, its darkened windows newly treacherous.

She only advertises in the Classifieds and only the ones where she need not list the price. She would have had to choose on eBay. She would have had to choose in *Auto Trader*. Only in the backs of the local papers can she find a place to list the sale without needing to state what it's worth.

She doesn't know what it's worth, that's the truth. Or why it's not worth exactly the same as it was when he carefully performed the three point turn that parked it where it stands now. She keeps it ticking over.

Where does it lose value? In the dust sown across the paintwork? Through the soft dark stain of exhaust across the concrete floor? If someone can tell her from where the value seeps, and at what rate, then she'll be able to tell them exactly what it's worth now.

She remembers how they sat there as he killed the ignition, his hand resting on the gear stick, the garage door open before them, showing a breadth of suburban, homely road. And the sound created by adjusting one's position on the seat, and the smell of the carpets – untouched by any other shoe. Her bag and his coat on the backseat behind them. His smile beneath the shadow of the garage roof.

Still the man wants it. He wants it despite the fact that he no longer trusts his own desire. But his wife now, his partner, she's crossed her own internal line. Nothing valuable ever comes at the buyer's price.

Helen watches her walk the herringbone brick driveway for the first time and step over the threshold into the garage. She does this in order to justify her change of mind, though she's not aware of why she does it. Helen knows her type only too well.

She says, 'I think if you expect to sell it, you need to be prepared to explain to people why it is you've never driven it yourself.'

Helen recalls the stockbroker's wife who'd stood approximately where this woman's standing now, younger, prettier, darker-haired, possessor of zero faux anythings, and how she'd come to the edge of the doorway, putting one hand out to assess the vehicle through her index fingertip, having performed every other test of which she'd been advised.

'I don't expect to sell it necessarily,' she answers quietly.

She doesn't want to admit to this woman – least of all a woman like this, and in front of this nice-seeming man – that she can't drive.

He told her he would take her to the beach, a beach that he knew well but that he hadn't seen himself for years, and they'd swap seats and she could jump and stall and lurch all she liked on the safe expanse of sand. They'd look up the time of year when low tide and twilight coincided.

He said he'd buy her weekly lessons. It was nothing, he said, by comparison he knew that, but nonetheless they'd be a gift from him. He said a large number of things that did not turn out to be true and she remembers every one of them she can.

She has been tempted to try to make it out to that beach herself, not to drive of course, but to walk there.

It's the name she can't remember. Regardless of the way she tries to retain things, some of them still seem to slip from her grasp.

Perhaps one day she'd still like to drive. Perhaps one day she'll still take lessons. It isn't as if his absence makes her incapable. Every third night she runs the vehicle to keep its engine working – sits for a while in the shadowed driver's seat herself. And she thinks about forwards movement, and she listens to the sounds of the new seats, the upholstery, smells the smell of this thing that could have been his. And she understands what it feels like to want to drive away somewhere. What it must be like to be this great big four by four, staring blind in the dusty dark morning after morning, at the indistinct lines of light around the garage door.

The couple who visited the car didn't travel far and so it's not long until they're home. At seven they eat. At nine they retire to the bedroom. He takes the left hand side of the bed and she takes the right. She can't sleep without adopting this arrangement.

They don't sleep yet of course, though with each year that passes they seem to do so at an earlier time. She lies beside him on the covers in her nightdress and the dark blue dressing gown that he bought for her, with sweeping kimono sleeves. Not a choice on his part, but a request on hers.

'I don't think the woman had her feet on the ground,' she resumes. 'If you ask me it was laughable. I mean what sort of person tries to sell a car like that? Or puts an advert in the paper when they don't even want to sell it *necessarily*? Maybe that's how she gets people to visit. She's desperate for company.'

He doesn't answer her.

He takes his book from the night table but in fact he doesn't want to read and he gazes at the changing pictures on the TV screen.

She says, 'How much do you think she paid for it? She obviously got it new. It must be more than twenty grand's worth in that garage. Well someone's bound to think it's a deal I suppose. Maybe someone who's good with mechanics. Can things go wrong on a car that's only driven five miles? It looked perfect. She obviously keeps it in running order. But I'm glad you didn't want the thing. I don't think I'd have wanted to get inside.'

'There wasn't anything wrong with it,' he says.

He regrets this though, because she begins to speak again. She talks about the smell of the vehicle. She talks about the way the woman watched him. 'She liked you,' she says. 'I could tell.' But she turns back and forth as she keeps talking, trying to exorcise this other woman – who he can tell she feels has in some way won – at no point does she ask him what figure he might have thought of offering. Or if he considered making the vehicle his at all.

He is himself under the bedcovers; newly changed bedcovers scented with the fabric softener she prefers. Numbers travel through his imagination: miniscule, exotic numbers. He holds his book. He looks at the TV screen.

The central heating is on its rounds again. It's hot already, surely hotter than it's meant to be – he turned down the thermostat only a week ago. But he can hear the water now, working its blunt head down the pipes, first from the kitchen where they're painted olive green, then through to the bedroom here, where they become cream like the vine-patterned paper, and thence into the radiators – already distended, scalding – fixed to every wall but the one against which his head now lies.

Birdfeed

The first cigarette of the day, guilty pleasure – not that it really matters anymore, benzene, nitrosamines, formaldehyde and hydrogen cyanide. The routine matters. The cup of tea and if they were to list what was in the teabag would it look like that list? Unintelligible reality underneath the friendliness of each brand's recognisable colour scheme. Cup of tea, first cigarette, the routine is the framework, preventing the hours from untying themselves and lying useless. He used to savour these moments when the rest of his time did not belong to him: take a break, smoke a fag, little five minute bubble. Now they are the measurements. Go to the shop. A morning's work. Nap the afternoon. An evening scheduled in the bright coded boxes of the *Radio Times* and a diary to mark appointments, bloodtest, physio.

Leila comes on Wednesday afternoons; Mark never comes. Mark is a digitised voice with the whitenoise of traffic, some road that can't be too far from this road. The same questions checklisted with open air in his tone, is the medication, have you had breakfast. Then the broad sweep of a life too full to be fully described, work, the girlfriend, the flat, the weather. Leila comes on Wednesday afternoons and seems proud of herself which allows her to be short-voiced, efficient. A lot of people aren't even having kids anymore; he doesn't have any grandchildren on the way. Fifty years' time what will they do? What will happen on their Wednesdays? The policy makers and think tanks must be shitting themselves.

She says, did you take a painkiller with that look that pretends not to judge. She says, only be a couple of days till the next injection.

Draw deep. *Fumar puede matar.* Cheap fags packed in someone's euro-sunlit backseat, crossing borders like swallows without knowing; sold four fifty for twenty at the bar in the Cross and exhausted, extinguished in his graveyard ashtray. The fags travel further than him.

He has a groundfloor flat so it's all good. He has a French window and a square of lawn and he's so close to the bus stop that their dragging engines punctuate his dreams. He does not yet need mobility aids. He has a long scarf tied around the French window's handle and he circles his body until it's wrapped around him, he pulls it open with the weight of himself.

She says, 'The room's there. It's got a nice view, you know.' Every culture has its 'you know.' It's rude in any culture not to ask for constant confirmation that your opinions are shared. The room has a ready made-up bed and a built-in cupboard. He can move in straight away at any time. The room is the very last place. That single bed where she now lets guests sleep.

Move the arm, first up then to the right, dying a mechanical death like all mechanical things, unnecessary these days, then down; tap the ash. Crystals are attacking his joints, his own immune system, but it's better than cancer she says. It's not Alzheimer's. He still knows who she is when she comes in.

When everyone from his generation is dead no one will say hello to anyone else in the high street any more. All the shopkeepers are from the Punjab. They think sycophancy is friendliness, and all the punters keep up the facade because that's multiculturalism in all its glory. The ability to smile at a face that doesn't look like yours. They don't know each other's names, their kids pass one another without recognition.

She comes to unroll the toilet paper for him on Wednesday afternoons. If he takes the room she'll be able to do it every day. Some machine out there somewhere, maybe in Thailand, designed to function without any break, rolling, rolling, until every soft absorbent strip is neatly packed into its circles. He buys it and she unrolls it for him. He is no longer able to take advantage of convenience.

There are dandelions in his ankle-deep lawn. His feet slush through grass. He has a birdtable and feeder. She doesn't help him maintain it – it's his to do every morning at ten o'clock. They rely on him. Where will they find wind-blown seed here? They look for cylindrical hanging cages in the atlas of back gardens, all planted with ready-made annuals, half-grown plugs bought in six-packs. It's dirt on the wind, carbon fumes that have coalesced. They occupy the trees as though above a flooded land.

Lift arm, up then right then down, tap ash, bring back to mouth.

It's spring. The municipal flowerbeds are undergoing their mid-season restock. Tulips and crocuses now.

But he never wanted to end up in the countryside. What would he be then, surrounded by nature, waiting to rejoin the chain. He'd rather be buried in a city cemetery, end to end and arm to arm with others. *Fumar puede matar.* Rather have unknown footsteps go past.

They've made something here haven't they. They've made a statement, shown what they can do, build neck-craning high and span rivers with beauty, make money, rotate it; they have taken the ground and drawn it into towers, found a career for every child. Cities aren't bad places. Human beings aren't bad animals. Just restless that's all.

Ten to ten. He keeps the seed in a cupboard above the sink. Everybody's scared of birdflu now. He reminds himself to wash his hands.

The cigarette end doesn't crush properly but lies insolent in the ashtray beside him. What does it mean, good for you and bad for you; how can they assess it? Where is their unchanging variable? Their control group? Even geography teachers know that statistics lie. He doesn't cough; his whole body is seizing into skeleton but his lungs sit strong and unafraid. They talk through their arses. Colonising advert breaks, using public money for educating people to live in the way that costs the state least. Don't take back pain lying down. Use the guidelines issued on how not to patronise those with mental health issues. Having trouble dealing with debt? The advert breaks are now a vein between the government and the community, pumping information one direction only. A million open-eyed and sucking without knowing it, suffused with facts they couldn't draw on if they tried, but facts that form the basis of their lives, underwrite the fears they can't define with a solid societal floor. No one's ever alone.

Leila and husband already have digital. They talk about programmes on BBC 7 but the name still sounds improbable to him. How can there be enough content? Perhaps digital snow forms islands between the property ladder programmes, or governmental health announcements.

He has not taken up Suduko.

He can't finish a crossword. Sometimes he considers waiting for the answers and then filling them into yesterday's boxes, just for a sense of completion. Closure the Americans say. It annoys him to see them unfinished.

He passes the annoyance onto her, small pleasures.

'What did they say about your results last Tuesday; how they looking?'

'Satisfaction, seven letters, ending e.'

'Because they said they were worse last week didn't they. Or have they lost them again.'

'Ending e, maybe fourth letter s; it's like a wall across the whole bottom corner. Come on, I thought you were clever.'

'You should have a go at them for it. Really, because they get away with it, then why should they care? Got to stamp your foot, Dad.'

'I can't stamp my foot.'

'Metaphorically speaking.'

'They can't hear me metaphorically stamp my foot. Closure.'

'Closure?'

'That's what the Americans say. Where's my pen?'

Fat pens, fat forks. Everything easy to use in his claw-fingered spas hands. He drops stuff all the time, doesn't even need to pick them up to drop them, the carpet's a silent haven for all the things he wants.

Ten o'clock. He puts his claws on the armrests of the chair. Folded spine, ready to uncrease to vertical, tensed thighs and stalled heart as he waits for the pain. Standing. Learning to stand again. In the spring quiet he cries out; it's his own home to cry out, no one winces and comes running, no one rushes to augment him with their flexible useful hands. Standing. It hurts like hell, like the damned must feel pain. One step forward.

He lives in a flat where the previous tenants left their lives in a grey film that coats the wallpaper dimmer, makes each window smaller, has worn the carpet slowly away. Ghosts of furniture in the places where the pile is still good. Memories of bookshelves on the walls. Blu-tack. There was a photo here once. Smiles sank and were embedded in the plasterwork. He has two chairs but no sofa and not enough plates to host a dinner party. None of the cupboard doors fit well. Machines can't do it all.

He takes the seed from the one above the sink and reminds himself to wash his hands. Bernard Matthews suffered an outbreak recently; it was all over the news, vacuum-formed turkey slice packets lay unbought for weeks underneath the ageless light of supermarket aisles. Happy smiling Bernard Matthews; the family brand. There are far more scares now. Scare has become a cultural climate, a new noun. But manufacturers are larger isn't it, foreign usually, and that half-formed noun is apt, disconnected, just filling the spaces between them all, infusing the air.

He isn't scared. He's scared of pain, the next movement, the moment he needs the next thing. But not generally scared. He's scared of his daughter's guest bedroom but he doesn't wake up in fear each day. That's what a lot of people do isn't it. He doesn't set an alarm clock anymore.

Turn the scarf around himself and put his heft against it – there's still enough of him to outweigh the double glazing and it slides with soulless ease. And the air is warm and all birds are crying morning spring, city spring, telecommunication from forsythia to forsythia: grub's up. The lawn is a viscous mass around his socks and sandals. Husband will come to mow it soon. He mows their own lawn twice a week she says. If he takes the room then grass will never trouble him again.

He used to be a delivery driver but not everyone can have an acting career can they, imagine a world like that and no one to buy the magazines. There's nothing to be ashamed of in a functional vocation. He never wanted to be a celebrity. The route was Hackney, Angel, King's Cross, sometimes west to Portobello. Cathy put notes by the side of his sandwiches with sweeter things than they talked about at home. For a while she was a receptionist, then a mum, then a dinner lady, her smile emerged from a face that grew older, each era spawned a different uniform. She finished crosswords, like the Jack Spratt ditty, they had interlocked.

He was never unfaithful except once, when she was threatening to leave him. He didn't enjoy it; the girl was attractive but she couldn't make him single or independent again, not even Cath leaving could have done that. She'd had peroxide hair, the girl. She'd said ooo. Now he enjoys the memory instead, they're no longer at odds, remembering the way Cath used to write Miss you, Love you and the way the girl conscientiously removed her tights. Faithfulness has fewer boundaries in retrospect. Maybe Cathy's looking down.

Place the seed bag on the table. Hold the feeder with the left hand; remove; remove the lid with the right; the lid and the feeder are attached to one another. Take hold of the seed bag, invert.

The sun makes his hands a different colour.

They are laying eggs now, all the birds. They're still having children.

He misses her now. He never did when he was working; he was embarrassed by the notes but now he understands their capital letters and their disregard for grammar; he Misses her. They'd borne each other out with love.

What did you do with your life? He can't help but ask himself.

And he tries to answer: I was a delivery driver. I was a father. I was a worker. I was a worthwhile man.

Anamorphosis

Time had gone by but Adam started to feel it wasn't healing him. Something wasn't right – anyway he had to make sure whether it was right or not. What he had to do, he started seeing, was clear this thing up. Sort it out once and for all.

He messaged Phil. Phil was her brother. He'd put up a new profile picture the week before. It was of him in San Francisco. He'd just got back.

How was San Francisco? Adam messaged. *Hows things in general? I'm surviving.☺ Same shit different day.*

Things looked like they were good for Phil. Phil was in a relationship now, he saw, with a girl called Lucy Bickerton, who was cute. She hung around with Kelly Newns it looked like, who'd always been hot. There was one picture of the two of them together – Lucy and Kelly Newns – at some kind of hen party or something, dressed as angels.

Phil messaged back: *Sweet Ad. U?*

There'd been a point when they'd been pretty tight, him and Phil. One time he'd even lent Phil seven hundred pounds before Christmas.

Ad asked for his phone number, or for his phone number again. In fact he'd thought he had it. Scrolling down, there was no Phil though. He must have changed phones since, and it was ages since he'd changed phones.

'How was San Francisco?' he went.

'Fucking amazing,' Phil said. It was Sunday; he was caned. You could hear it.

'You cross that bridge?' Ad asked him.

'Fucking right,' Phil said.

'Working or playing?'

'Both, man.'

It was trimming season in California.

'What can I do for you Ad?' Phil asked him.

It must have been '08, that Christmas when he'd lent him the money. Phil had just lost his job at Richer Sounds. He'd paid him back though. He'd got a job that March again, out at the Comet in Bluewater, where it was better commission anyway, or that's what Phil had said.

Ad told Phil what he could do: he said he needed Evvy's address. He said he still had a box of her stuff, and that things had settled now, and he knew she'd want it back.

Google streetview could look into her road. Her garden was small, no uglier or prettier than any of the others.

She was living out in the suburbs now. The house was a new build, yellow brick. The road was a cul-de-sac.

Most of what he could see had been a year ago; the image date was January '09. He moved up and down the surrounding roads and returned to hers. This year it had been wet and grey. There'd been very few days like the day pictured: clear, when you got that silence and winter offered that electric blue sky above a stationary kind of world.

'So are you alright man?' Phil had asked at the end of their conversation on the phone. And Ad had told him it wasn't a problem. That he was glad about the way it had worked out in the end. He hadn't finished living his life yet, he said, which felt true now that he was going back to put it all to rest.

He tried to place her in the streetview. In his mind's eye he tried to put her on the path with a pushchair, both her and the kid bundled up in coats. She'd used to wear a big puffa coat. He imagined the sort of boots she'd have. But he couldn't picture it clearly enough to summon the features of her face, let alone see beneath the hood to conjure up the child's.

Change is on its way, he updated his status and, when two friends commented asking what, just responded that he mustn't open his mouth yet. But he was aware of the weight suddenly, now that he was making moves towards shedding it – aware of how heavily it had been lying – and he could not resist posting something about how he felt.

He raised a sash window despite the cold to let the view and any passing conversation in. Stood smoking a spliff, the car park below displaying shoppers and traffic, people all trying to go about their lives. He remembered feeling isolated from everyone that morning – sitting struck dumb in the crowd – but in reality he wasn't on his own.

He'd been doing building work on the Underground so it had been daytime; it had always been daytime when they'd seen each other. Probably that had made it easier for her. Also it had put him out of kilter with the world such as it was rolling out in front of him now.

They'd gone out. She'd wanted to go out; he remembered turning up at her door and being knackered and not wanting to go anywhere except her bed and her saying, 'We never go out.' But where was open in the daytime? They'd ended up in a café.

What she'd needed actually – this he'd realised halfway through – was to go somewhere he couldn't kick off. She'd sat there telling him and all he'd been able to think was, he couldn't shout, or tell her what he felt, or what he thought of her, or anything.

He'd gone to work that night – he remembered descending with the lift, the Northern Line he'd been working on – he remembered standing there staring at the back of everyone else's heads and encountering vivid pictures of all the things he hadn't been able to do.

On Tuesday he travelled to see her. He took the bus through the long cold winter afternoon.

Golders Green was an animalarium, everyone running tense, all of them ridden by the cold.

His reflection was transient as the bus passed anything darker than the sky. He tried to see himself, first of all like she would, then like one of these people. He tried to guess his own job. He guessed at his age. He saw a young woman with her hand on a pram and an African mama in gold.

He didn't have any desire to attract Evvy again, but still the clothes he'd chosen were ones she'd used to find attractive. He'd put on shoes instead of trainers and his best shirt – had carefully worked the collars and cuffs into place until, outwardly, he'd been ready to go and had stood, fingering the buttons, smoothing the shirt, less and less certain of himself within it.

This was the problem: he didn't know whether or not he was in debt. A person couldn't go around carrying something like that, which might or might not be a burden. A person needed to be able to look in the mirror and believe in what they saw.

Evvy had blue eyes, much like Ad himself. Sometimes, out and about together, in queues, in shops, strangers had asked whether they were siblings. They had laughed. They had said, 'My God I hope not.' They had kissed to demonstrate their actual relationship.

They'd been an attractive couple. Strangers had said this too.

Preparing to leave, he examined his face for transformation. He was still young, as was she. But he saw changes. And growing consistencies too – as the puppy fat began to disappear from his features, genetic characteristics showing through.

Was it the same with personalities?

'There's a lot of things I have to take into consideration,' she'd explained to him in the cafe that day. She had held her mug of tea with both hands on the surface of the table, her similar blue eyes trying, despite their tears, to evaluate him objectively.

He disembarked at Lender Close like Phil had told him. Number 17 was visible from where he stepped down. For a while he did nothing but remained at the bus stop, sitting on the sloped yellow plastic as if waiting to be taken away again.

He wasn't going to fuck up her life.

He smoked three cigarettes. Buses did come and go.

He was here, but he wouldn't approach the place if her boyfriend was in. Nor would he if he couldn't tell.

Not yet captured by Google, in real life the house had been newly painted; the window frames and front door blue instead of white. Early dark started muffling the street. First one window and then another was lit.

He thought about Kelly Newns, who didn't even look any different. A Sales Progressor at Barnard Marcus now he'd seen. He had trawled her visible albums for photos tagged with Evvy, but either they didn't hang out anymore or the albums were hidden from him.

Evalina didn't have an account. Or, if she had an account, it wasn't one that he'd been able to find.

Adam sat through one more drop-off, a greater number of passengers released onto the pavement, an old man with a tie gazing at him from the bus's window as he failed to get in and ride away.

244

Individually the streetlamps began to come on.

He had sat looking at his own profile a lot recently too – his profile as it was seen by all his friends, because he didn't use the privacy settings; didn't have anything to hide. And yet that wasn't how it had felt, open or honest like *he* was open and honest. He'd seen a lie in it, in his pictures, his info, everywhere, a lie by omission, which was what he felt inside himself.

First she'd told him she was pregnant, then she'd told him that she was still having sex with her ex-boyfriend. Not very often, she'd said, just now and then.

'Well whose baby do you think it is?' he'd asked her.

But she hadn't had any answer. It was the strangest thing. He remembered sitting immobile between the cafe's many lunchtime sounds – to be delivered this news, which might or might not make him a father. It wasn't even the betrayal of it necessarily, but the absence of clear knowledge, which had taken root in him.

'Well whose baby do you want it to be?' he'd said eventually, which was when she'd told him about how there were all these things, the ones she had to consider. She had continued crying, in silence because of course they'd been in public, and without ever taking those blue eyes off him. Not one reaction had passed through his heart that she hadn't been able to see.

'Whose baby do *you* want it to be?' she had asked him in return.

In the lower lit window of the house on Lender Close, a man came into view.

Ad watched his silhouette, moving ordinarily around their living room. It looked as if he had dark hair. It looked as if they were about the same age.

As Adam watched, the front door opened and this man appeared. He trotted down the steps shouldering his coat, made brief eye contact, got into the white hatchback opposite and drove away.

Adam stood as the taillights fled the street. He wondered at this coincidence.

As he'd been unable to do in Google streetview, he approached the house.

There was this sensation, of the parts of his life in motion. This possibility of things falling into place. A tricycle stood pushed back against the wall, its wheel skewed by the line of the chain-link fence.

The woman who opened the door had a towel in one hand and the rest of the evening slung across her face. She said nothing as she recognised him. There was no sound of a television or radio from inside.

Adam saw how much weight she'd lost.

'I didn't want to call in case he answered. I'm not here to cause any problems. Sorry.'

The corridor was dim, the only light coming from the kitchen some way behind her, but it was clear how much she'd changed. She wasn't looking after herself. She had no make up on and her hair was greasy, scraped back, but it was neither of these things entirely. It was in the way that she opened the door; the way her fingers held the frame.

'I waited till I saw him go...'

'What do you want Ad?'

'I need to come in. Like I'm not here to give you shit. I don't want to rock the boat.'

'You can't see it. It's asleep.'

'I don't have to see it. I just want to talk.' She didn't remove her arm from the door, standing there as if she was guarding the child against him, but he gained the impression that this was not what she was doing. 'How long's he gone for? You don't even want to tell me if it's a boy or a girl?'

A staircase led, gated, to a few visible feet of carpeted hallway above.

She saw his gaze climb them. 'It's not yours.'

'Are you sure? What do you mean? What just like that?' He laughed. His laughter left him. 'You mean it looks like him?'

'I had it tested.'

Words failed him for a moment. 'Are you sure?' he asked again. He examined her shut face. 'Are you alright Evvy?' he asked her. 'Let me in.'

There had been three envelopes: a pink, a yellow and a blue.

Big Brother had been on the television. Strains of silence from the *Big Brother* house had filtered through this house. The scent of sleep had filled the nursery.

You had to swab from the back of the mouth, the instructions had told her clearly; from the inside of the cheek.

'I came to try and do the right thing.' But as he said so,

247

he lost faith in this. 'I could just give you twenty, thirty quid a week. How certain is it, that kind of test?'

She had put the three attractively coloured envelopes into the larger one provided. She had put this in the back of the buggy. She had walked to the postbox and from there to the park, where November had ushered grey wind between the railings, and she'd sat and bounced the buggy up and down.

Silence contaminated the cold between them.

'Well I came back to check,' he said, but then he shouted, 'Fuck! Fuck, Evvy! *Fuck!* Well whatever. It's not mine.' He turned away from her a little. He hadn't meant to shout. 'Why don't you have Facebook?' he heard himself asking, empty, distraught. 'I wouldn't have needed to come.'

There were far fewer passengers on the bus home. He wasn't crying – he looked normal – but he stood holding onto the safety bar, feeling a hole inside himself, unbeknownst to the strangers he was surrounded by.

His reflection was continuous now, as were all of theirs. He saw a young girl talking to her mother but looking into the blackened glass instead, animated, watching herself speak in dedicated performance.

In her own kitchen again, Evvy washed her face over the remaining dishes and dried it on the towel she still held in her hands.

Holding the edges of the sink, she remained motionless as, from the baby monitor, the first rustle of movement for over an hour arrived. Seconds passed and it continued so that she was caused to look at it.

In the nursery upstairs, experiencing silence in its home again, the child had opened its ordinary eyes.

These Lights
However

Jim came to his own front door and knocked on it like a stranger.

He stood beneath the automatic wash of the security lamp, no laptop bag on his shoulder, no keys in his hand and no car in the driveway behind him. Regardless of these differences, the door looked just the same. To its right, at shoulder height, their oval brass plaque was still engraved 72.

He was cold. Seeing the line of light changing at the edges of the doorframe as his wife made her way down the corridor, the word *disorientated* occurred and recurred, but it was not the right word.

They'd bought the plaque at the Ortons garden centre; he remembered queuing with it under his arm. The door opened with its precise sounds, latch and Yale.

She recognised him instantly but whatever it was about him, which wasn't disorientation, took an instant longer for her to see – a flutter somewhere behind her evening face – a stutter.

'Jimmy,' she said, 'what's wrong?'

And though he knew with adequate clarity the course of events, he found himself unable to articulate them, not with the speed, the correct order necessary to stunt the progression of that fluttering into a look of full-blown fear.

She repeated the question but perhaps there was no comprehensive answer as he could relay the facts but they would not explain this situation – of her husband standing separate before his own doorstep with cold and shaking purple hands.

The leaves had risen toward his windscreen in an updraft from the dark. Into the path of the BMW, this he remembered. Revolving in the headlamps, broad hand-shaped leaves that were what – sycamore – unfurling.

'I love you,' he told her, when they were only halfway down the corridor.

The carpet was cream. She returned the words willingly, laying her hands on him, taking him to the sofa before letting her questions loose. The carpet was cream, the shadows gifted it varying colours though, blues and browns, which revealed themselves as he passed them.

The television in the living room was on standby. He watched its red light remain unchanging as he sat where she placed him, in the deep firm hold of the couch. She talked about making him tea with anxiety as the television's low frequency standby played under the silence of the room.

He had been in third, going uphill.

'I had a collision,' he said.

'Oh *no*. Jimmy, are you hurt? Are you ok? What happened? Tell me.' She took his hand and seemed briefly to examine it, causing him to follow her gaze over the slim veins and tendons that constituted it.

'The car is dead,' he told her.

In the soft familiarity of their living room, he raised his eyes and saw her face: her pretty aging eyes and clean hair, her half-worn shade of lipstick.

'What did you hit?' she asked him, as if the car mattered nothing.

'I don't know,' he responded slowly. 'A tree? I lost control.'

On the arm of the sofa next to him the television's remote control lay. A brushed chrome finish with a very few multifunctional buttons, arranged ergonomically and aesthetically, in crescent shape. Beyond her right shoulder he noticed the sound system, also on standby of course. And the warmth of the house, circulating at perfect regulatory pace, filling each of the radiators, here and in every room upstairs.

'Where's the car Jimmy? Did you leave it? Did you call anyone?'

'No. I should call.'

'Where did it happen? I'll call.'

'After the garage, on the backroad.'

'OK, I'll make you a nice cup of tea OK?'

She began to rise and he moved his fingers around her wrist to prevent her, whereupon she sat again, only looked at him, waiting for his words. But he couldn't take her back to that moment with him, to feel the airbag

252

engulfing them together, to experience the world rolling around the BMW as the car had given its life for his.

'Tell me,' she encouraged him.

But despite their twenty five years of marriage, and many shared silences, nothing could now be communicated to her, nothing of what he felt. The car had not burnt. Without an explosion, the night had descended to lie thickly in its folds of metal and its broken glass. As he had opened its unsound door and relieved himself of its embrace, tiny fragments of its windows had fallen with the ticking sounds of sleet. And he had stood alive in the wet leaves, not in darkness, because its headlamps had endured.

The tea cooled in its cup and he drank little. She led him upstairs for a bath. As she ran it, at its thermostatically determined temperature, she made the call in the study next door, on occasion peering around the wall to check facts with him or perhaps just to check on him in a general way. Bubbles rose in the water, real bubbles. He failed to undress.

He went to stand next to her. On their Dell PC screensaver, digital bubbles slipped across the monitor and rebounded from its borders, which they must have sensed and recognised. She saw him watching them without expression and, as she talked, placed one hand against his face.

He remembered the rising leaves, their colours in the headlamps, fragile things that could not cause damage. It had been his speed, his ease and complacency. It had been his fault.

After a short time the conversation ended with the person on the other end of the line.

'You're not hurt,' she prompted him, 'and you didn't hit anyone; it's OK.'

Behind her back, the high resolution bubbles went on and on.

She left him and turned the bath tap off.

'Thank God it's OK,' she said.

Yes, the radio had been on. It had been his ease and his complacency, singing; the radio had played. And leaves had risen in the updraft, rhythmical, in the soft and menacing organ tones of Marvin Gaye's *I Heard it Through the Grapevine*. The BMW's noise reduction had blocked out the reality of the night.

She had wanted a BMW. If he was honest – if life allowed you to play – he was a classic car man. Aesthetically, he leaned toward the 1940s. All new cars seemed slightly soulless.

In fact, it was she who had cried on every occasion that they'd changed cars. She'd loved their very first, a Morris Ital Estate with pale peppermint bodywork. She'd loved the Rover 214 that had taken them through the early nineties, and had begged him to maintain instead of exchange it. The car previous to the BMW had been an Audi A4. When they'd bought it, their first trip had been to Norfolk and every country lane had made her wince.

He wasn't a sentimental man, though he had always tried not to belittle sentimentality on her part. Now though, one evening returned to his mind. Her gallbladder operation; also an autumn night, coming back from the hospital after she'd awoken. He had taken one of their spare blankets from the cupboard she kept above the wardrobe in the guest room, and she'd accepted it after getting seated comfortably in the car. Not something necessary maybe, but something appreciated. He remembered driving back, cresting the motorway junction, with the intricacies of the city lights becoming visible in front, penetrating the darkened BMW's interior to reveal her, leaning her head against the passenger windowpane.

He'd seen a television programme recently following the evolution of electricity. The advent of vacuum cleaners, it had said, washing machines, televisions, automatic juicers, all such things, could be traced back to one imbalance. Electric lighting was only needed at night. A tremendous infrastructure had been required to provide these lights however. It had been essential to ensure that the electricity, which could not be turned off, was drawn from the sockets, paid for and utilised during the hours when the sun still shone.

Jim stood in front of their screensaver, watching it as if for the first time. He remembered gearing down. Technology thrives by restructuring its environment. This was what the programme had said.

'Come on Jimmy.' She put her hand into the crook of his arm, 'Come on and get in.'

The PC was not online. The broadband sat primed, awaiting.

There were such things, Jim thought suddenly, as emotional hyperlinks. Like the other evening when they'd been watching TV, some makeover programme that she enjoyed. And the stylist had talked about how important it was to change your hair parting on a regular basis. He hadn't changed his parting for years – perhaps never – and all at once he'd been worried about baldness. Insecure and prematurely old.

Like the web, but inside you, there were such things as emotional hyperlinks.

Seeing him unmoving, Cath busily began to shut the computer down.

Look, he wanted to say. Look at how the mouse fits to your hand.

But instead he told her, 'The car is dead.'

And she did attempt to reassure him, pointing out that the BMW was not a human being – that the events of the last two hours could have been much worse. But watching Windows shutting down, saving his settings, he was suddenly aware of a rush of love for the system: cradling his Word docs and his JPEGs, enabling him. In its final moments, he thought, the car had activated its ABS.

He was conscious of the radio's electrohum as she led him past it into the light, though it was off – he checked to make sure. But it seemed to give voice to the air with its unchanging digital sleepsong, denoting information highways that remained unseen.

Maputo. Low Season

Scene from the global village: Man suspected of intent to robbery gunned down in Maputo street. Low season.

Everywhere I go with my white face sewn onto me. Looking out of tinted hotel window at dead boy. Or what – young man – early twenties. From the back of the head you can't really tell.

He lies there still caught in a posture that's ready to run. People walk a wide radius, taking photos with their mobile phones and digital cameras. Aren't you surprised, another traveller had asked me, by how many of these Africans have mobile phones? The walls of Mozambique tropical yellow and blue with M-Cell and Vodacom signs. People walk a pie chart round him, while his blood – which does not look red but purple – makes its way away. Finds the lowest path of the gutter where last night thunderstorms really had filled the potholes with rain.

Not much blood for a death. And his arms bent at the elbows – face-down – and white trainers toe-down on the tarmac. Guards idle at the corners of the empty space that he now keeps around him, AK47s awkward to hold in one hand, but not casual enough in two.

At first he didn't die. They came back to kill him. My husband saw it while I was still dressing – the boy moving blearily, pinned by his injuries, he says. He does not move now, not in all the time I stand and look. And where are the other four? Five men the hotel staff say. Where are his optimistic comrades? Where are the other four bodies?

The traffic continues through the junction; each car on safari through this scene. And my husband and I prepare our bags and walk downstairs to check out of Hotel 2001. Humid sun. The smell of rubbish. Everyone seeing the same eight runners emerging where his chest meets the road. He hadn't planned on dying but absconding. Dressed in his best T shirt and jeans he'd planned on escape through these streets. The crowd not making crowd noises now the gunshots are finished, just this multicoloured mill of every face turned towards the same place. They don't comment with any volume but I see one man gesture explanations to another of the movements that had ended in that spot.

Children stand with hands on hips. They don't cry and certainly don't turn their eyes away, because when you see it, it's just a dead body – a boy, a young man – who's been caught. And most passing things at the road go on the same.

Everywhere, I am an English girl with an Afrikaner husband. Everywhere we go, we say we come from Wales. In a restaurant in Swaziland, we met a young Dlamini. Ate roast pork shoulder together and talked politics in a land where everything's so cheap it's free.

In Maputo rubbish swims the streets and buttresses walls. People have made landfill sites on the hills outside their doors. In other parts of Mozambique, chickens stalk the garbage territories, but here there are no chickens. On a roundabout as you enter the city, in the runnels of the rubbish, three men are washing something in the brown water that spills from the mouth of a pipe.

The softchewed matchstick between the teeth. How long would they leave the boy there?

They have to accept tourists into their world, in order to open the gates to what they bring. All these men held guns when they were boys and without them now there's no work left. Agricultural ground, an investor told us, one dollar per hectare inland.

As we wait, bus drivers call their destinations: Mbabane, Nelspruit, last board. The decks and cranes of passing ships are visible between the buildings. Maputo owns the largest harbour in Southern Africa – not Cape Town.

We sit and wait four hours before another sixteen passengers can be gathered. We eat chicken and throw the polystyrene box into the treasure of rubbish outside. Moments later I watch a pedestrian pick it up and walk keenly away but I don't mention this to the man I love.

The rain begins to fill the street again. Flowering trees in the centre of drunken roads, pavements gone. One line of faded hazard tape redirects the traffic. How long would they leave the boy there? Cooler boxes displaying Fanta and Coke, biscuits and soap powder, gin, black diesel smoke from the heaving chapa engines coaxed into one more trip, one more day in which we hope to leave. Samosas in oil-filled Tupperware boxes. Our bags clutched or tied to us, our money stashed. And washing-up bowls of bread on the heads of women who squint through the brightness towards another sale. The sale of everything – display boards made of sticks and flattened cardboard boxes, fabric in Technicolor prints and cheap nail varnish. Everything offered in through the window we look out of. Special price, good price. Everywhere, with my white face.

Scene from the global village – Maputo. Low season.

Bananas, pinstripe suits, pay as you go airtime. I tell them over and over – in my bad Spanish though they speak Portuguese – that I don't want it. Not a coconut, or a bottle of water, or a single gold chain held over the run of four knuckles.

Short

For several weeks in Archway, where no homeless person stays too long, there was a man living under a red blanket. He just lay underneath it most of the time; he was right at the end of the line. He had a terribly swollen head and this red face and he didn't seem to know where he was. The blanket was thin and obviously dirty. They were there together all day, all night. I don't know what happened to the man. One morning I saw the blanket on its own in the rubbish beside the road, still bright red despite everything.

Acknowledgements

'Recreation' was published in a prior form as 'I Can Hear the Grass Grow' in *Perverted by Language*, edited by Peter Wild.

'We Wanted To Give You Something' was published in a prior form as 'Lovers' in *All Hail the New Puritans*, edited by Matt Thorne and Nicholas Blincoe.

For the love and happiness in my life, thank you both so much, Ken and Woefie.

Thanks to my parents, as always, without whose encouragement I'd never have been able to begin. Thank you to Lucy Luck, for your constant support and dedication. And to Kathryn Gray, for giving me confidence again.

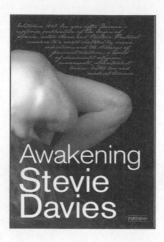

Awakening
Stevie Davies

'Carries an impressive deal of intensive research lightly ... the portraiture throughout is graphic, richly detailed and subtly shaded'
New Welsh Review

Dream On
Dai Smith

PARTHIAN

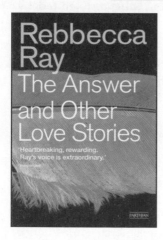

Rebbecca Ray
The Answer and Other Love Stories

'Heartbreaking, rewarding. Ray's voice is extraordinary.'

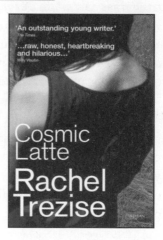

'An outstanding young writer.'
The Times

'...raw, honest, heartbreaking and hilarious...'
Willy Vlautin

Cosmic Latte
Rachel Trezise

www.parthianbooks.com